# 5-Minute
# BUNNY TALES
## for
# Bedtime

Illustrated by Peter Stevenson
Stories by Sally Sheringham and Joan Stimson

· Derrydale Books ·
New York

First published in Great Britain in 1989 by
The Paul Hamlyn Publishing Group Limited
a Division of Reed International Books Limited
Michelin House, 81 Fulham Road, London SW3 6RB

Story writers: Joan Stimson, Sally Sheringham

This 1991 edition published by Derrydale Books,
distributed by Outlet Book Company, Inc.,  ·
a Random House Company,
225 Park Avenue South,
New York, New York 10003.

Printed and bound in Italy

ISBN 0-517-66471-2

8765432

**G**regory had earache. Doctor Dogood gave him some special ointment. His mother rubbed in the ointment gently. Then she stuffed Gregory's ears with cotton balls.

Gregory soon felt better. But he couldn't hear anything.

"EAT YOUR SUPPER, DEAR," shouted his mother at supper time.

"BRUSH YOUR TEETH," called his father, afterwards.

"MOVE OVER, GREGORY," bellowed his brothers and sisters at bathtime.

"What about a story?" asked Gregory at bedtime.

"THAT'S GOING TO BE DIFFICULT," agreed his Mom and Dad. "WE CAN'T SHOUT A WHOLE STORY."

They decided that Gregory's brothers and sisters would have to amuse him instead.

Michael juggled with some carrots.

Gina did a ballet dance.

Tommy rode around the bed on his scooter.

Susan stood on her head and put her tongue out.

Gregory clapped and laughed. "THIS IS EVEN BETTER THAN A STORY," he shouted to his family.

The Harum-Scarums were taking a bath.

"Let's wash our ears first," said Jason. "We'll do each others.' It's more fun that way."

The Harum-Scarums clambered about, making great big waves in the tub.

"Let's pour in some more bath foam," said Molly.

They whooped and splashed, to make the bubbles even bigger.

"Let's wash our toes next," said Jill.

The Harum-Scarums laughed and kicked as they washed their toes.

"Let's run some more water," said Gordon. "There doesn't seem to be much left in here."

Suddenly, Mrs. Harum-Scarum burst into the bathroom. There was Jason with soap in his eye, Jill with bubbles in her ears, Gordon with his toe stuck in the drain, and Molly and her duck floating across the floor.

"Oh, no!" she exclaimed. "I'll have to get a snorkel and flippers to sort all this out!"

**H**ugh's parents had gone out for the evening. Aunt Mildred was babysitting.

Hugh didn't like Aunt Mildred. She always wore a big hat, and she had a loud voice. Sometimes she gave Hugh a big hug. He didn't like that either.

"Time for bed," boomed Aunt Mildred.

Hugh leapt upstairs, took a shower and brushed his teeth. Then he chose a book to read. He didn't want any auntie reading to *him*. Then he climbed into bed.

Suddenly Hugh cried, "HELP, HELP," at the top of his voice.

Aunt Mildred rushed upstairs. "What is it?" she boomed.

"There's a SPIDER in my bed," sobbed Hugh.

"Never mind," said Aunt Mildred.

She took off her hat, popped the spider inside, and took it down to the garden.

When she returned, Hugh was very relieved.

"What about a story?" she said.

"Oh, yes *please*, Aunt Mildred," replied Hugh. "And I wouldn't mind a hug first!"

# R

achel Rabbit put on her new witch's outfit. Then she crept up behind her friends, waved her magic wand and cried in a witchlike voice: "I'm going to cast a spell on you!"

"We know it's you, Rachel," they laughed, because under the black hat they recognized her nose and whiskers. "You can't scare us."

Just then, Farmer Potatoes came up. He looked very sad. "The crows are eating all my corn," he said. "My scarecrows don't seem to scare them any more."

"I bet *I* can scare the crows," said Rachel, excitedly.

The crows were most alarmed to see an evil-looking witch running toward them waving her magic wand. And when they heard her cackle, "Hubble, bubble, blood and bone, any crow I see I will turn to stone," they flew away in fright, never to be seen again.

Farmer Potatoes was so grateful to Rachel he gave her the biggest, juiciest bunch of carrots she had ever seen.

**M**olly's sister was very bossy. Every time Molly picked up a toy, her sister said *she* wanted to play with it. Whenever Molly wanted to play "going to the beach," Molly's sister said *she* wanted to play something else.

"I'm going to read a book in my bedroom," said Molly one day.

"You can't," said Molly's sister. "*I* want to read that book."

"OK," said Molly. "I'll go outside and play instead."

Molly went outside, and began to play in the sandbox.

Molly's sister could see Molly playing happily outside. She wished she could play outside with Molly. "Can I play with you?" she called from the window. "I promise I won't be bossy."

"Oh, yes please!" called Molly to her sister.

And together, they made the biggest sand castle you ever saw.

**M**elvyn zippered up his spacesuit. It came right up under his chin. It gave him a nice, secure feeling. He fastened his helmet. It was almost time for lift-off.

TEN close the spaceship doors, and counting

NINE check the door locks, and counting

EIGHT close the spaceship windows, and counting

SEVEN check the window locks, and counting

SIX check the control panel, and counting

FIVE check the Moon map, and counting

FOUR check the rocket boosters, and counting

THREE check the air supply, and counting

TWO take one last look at Earth, and counting

ONE ..... "SUPPER'S READY, MELVYN." Mom's voice rang clearly up the staircase.

Melvyn raced downstairs, two steps at a time. He didn't stop to count. Carrotburgers were more important than a trip to the Moon!

**S**idney had been to the dentist. The dentist had put on braces.

The dentist said it would make Sidney's front teeth straight. Sidney would grow into a handsome buck rabbit — without buck teeth.

Sidney was shy about his braces. He didn't want to talk; he didn't want to smile; he didn't want *anyone* to see his braces.

But when Sidney stopped talking and smiling, his brothers and sisters forgot he was there.

Sidney hopped off unhappily. "I'll just have to play by myself," he thought.

He came to a clearing in the wood. On the other side of the clearing was another rabbit. She was picking clover and humming a tune.

"That looks like Nancy," said Sidney to himself. "I'll go and surprise her."

Nancy heard soft hopping noises behind her. She turned around. Her face lit up when she saw Sidney. She smiled broadly.

Sidney smiled back at Nancy. He didn't mind smiling now — because Nancy had braces too!

**B**obby and Tom didn't want to go to sleep. They wanted to stay up and play with their toys.

"You can play again tomorrow," said their father. "Now it's time to sleep."

After a few minutes in bed, Tom opened his eyes. "Is it tomorrow yet?" he said.

"No, it isn't," said Bobby. "It's still dark. Go to sleep."

Later, Tom opened his eyes again. "It must be tomorrow by now," he thought. And he climbed out of bed.

Tom crept into the playroom. His toys were still there, just as he had left them. He played and played.

Soon, Tom began to yawn. "I think I'll have a little rest," he said, and he lay down next to his panda.

When Bobby came down in the morning, he found Tom lying on the playroom floor with his panda — fast asleep!

**G**erry had some new jeans. They were very, very tight, and very, very uncomfortable, but Gerry's mother wanted him to wear them right away.

Gerry went out to play. All his friends admired his jeans.

But when his friends asked him to play marbles with them and Gerry tried to bend down, his jeans were too tight. They wouldn't bend with him. He had to stand and watch the others play.

"Let's play football now," said his friends. They ran up and down the yard. But Gerry could only take tiny steps and soon no one wanted him on their team.

"Let's play hide-and-seek," said Gerry, who was beginning to get fed up.

But Gerry couldn't hide, because he couldn't crouch down.

Gerry went home in tears. His mother smiled kindly. "Let's go and get you a new pair of jeans," she said. "We can buy some bigger ones, and this time we'll make sure there's plenty of room — for when you grow bigger!"

**P**eggy was at the beach. The beach is meant to be fun, but Peggy was fed up.

First she built a sand castle, but the tide came in and the waves washed it all away.

"I want to go home," cried Peggy.

Then Peggy had an ice cream cone. But before she could eat it, the top fell off into the sand.

"I want to go home," sobbed Peggy.

Peggy bounced her beach ball. Suddenly, the wind caught it. It blew far out to sea.

"I want to go home," wailed Peggy.

Peggy's parents were snoozing on the beach. "We'll have to do something about Peggy," they agreed.

Peggy's father walked along the beach toward Peggy. Peggy was still sobbing.

"I want to ....." she began, but Dad interrupted her.

"Do you want a ride on a pedal boat?" he asked.

"Yes, please!" said Peggy. And suddenly, the beach was the most fun place in all the world.

**B**rian Bunny was exceedingly proud of his tail. He was forever combing it and crimping it and curling it and preening it.

"My tail is the whitest, fluffiest, finest tail in the whole warren," he would brag to the other rabbits. "Just look at your miserable-looking specimens! Compared to mine, yours are mere rats' tails!"

The rabbits grew extremely tired of Brian's boasting, but there was nothing they could do to stop him.

One day, Brian was looking over his shoulder to admire his tail in the reflection in the village pond. To get a better view he leant back a little bit further ... and a little bit further ... then — SPLASH! Aaah!

A very wet, embarrassed Brian Rabbit crawled out of the pond, dragging his bedraggled tail behind him.

The other rabbits couldn't stop laughing. "Whose tail looks like a rat's now!" they cried.

After that, Brian didn't boast about his tail ever again.

T he rabbits were having their annual sports day. Poor Walter had broken his leg. He couldn't run or jump. He could only hop along on crutches. It wasn't much fun just watching his friends.

Mr. Brown, the organizer, was calling out the order of the races on his megaphone. The rabbits listened carefully to hear their names.

"And now for the specialty race," boomed Mr. Brown.

The rabbits looked curious. They hadn't practised for any *specialty* race. Then, Walter heard his name being called.

He hopped forward.

Mr. Brown lined up the other rabbits in pairs. He tied together the two middle legs from each pair of rabbits. "That should slow them down a bit," he thought.

Mr. Brown blew his whistle.

What a muddle those rabbits got into! But Walter soon reached the winning post and won the race!

"Never mind," said Walter to the other rabbits. "You haven't had as much practice as I have. Now you know what it's like to run on crutches!"

**F**lorence had a floppy ear.

Her parents said it didn't matter. But it mattered to Florence. She would lie awake at night, wondering what to do about it.

One night, she slept with a book on her ear to make it straight. But as soon as she took the book away, her ear curled up again.

Another time she bound her ear with ribbons. That made her ear very straight. But in the morning, when she untied the ribbons, her ear curled up again.

Florence made her parents take her to the doctor. The doctor didn't have any cream for straightening ears.

"Don't worry," he said. "Young buck rabbits like girl rabbits with floppy ears."

Florence didn't believe him.

Valentine's day came. Florence knew she wouldn't get a Valentine card. But she was wrong . . .

PLOP! A big box came through the door.

Inside the box was a card, with a verse on it. This is what it said:

> "Roses are red,
> Violets are blue,
> FLOPPY EAR,
> I do love you!"

P eggy and Tom were heading off to sail around the world in a little wooden tub. They waved and waved until the harbor, the lighthouse, and their friends were just a tiny blur. "Now we're all alone," said Tom.

"Oh no we're not," cried Peggy. "Look behind you." And there was a huge shark with sharp teeth. If a school of fish hadn't suddenly appeared, Peggy, Tom and the tub would have almost certainly ended up in the shark's tummy!

They had just recovered from that narrow escape when a terrible storm started. It tossed the little tub hither and thither as if it were a ball. Peggy and Tom were very frightened — and also very seasick.

At last all was calm — and there, way off, they could see land!

"Our first desert island," cried Tom.

"Let's hope there aren't any cannibals," said Peggy.

But . . . surely a desert island shouldn't have a lighthouse and a harbor? They had done a complete circle and were back home again!

"Next time we'll take a compass with us," laughed Tom.

"And a real boat," added Peggy.

One morning, Topsy woke up feeling very peculiar. She got out of bed feeling very wobbly, and went to the bathroom feeling very hot and faint.

When she looked in the mirror, she had the shock of her life. Her face was covered in huge, red spots. And not only that, they were itching like mad!

Topsy didn't know what to do. She'd never had spots like this before. Perhaps something had happened to her in the night, she thought. Perhaps a wicked witch had put a magic spell on her? Perhaps she was turning into a strawberry? It was all very worrying.

Mrs. Bunny appeared at the bathroom door.

"Mommy, mommy, something terrible has happened to me," cried Topsy. "What am I going to do?

Mrs. Bunny laughed. "You are a silly bunny," she said. "You've got measles!"

And poor Topsy Bunny had to spend two weeks in bed before she was allowed to go out again.

# THE SNAKE CHARMER

**R**aj Rabbit went to the pet store and bought a snake. He called him Ramjam.

Raj decided to charm Ramjam. He would play some music and make him stand up in his basket.

Raj took his flute and began to play an old East-Indian tune.

He looked down hopefully into the basket. But Ramjam hadn't moved. He was still fast asleep.

Raj took a deep breath and blew right into the basket. Ramjam opened one sleepy eye and shut it again. But he didn't budge an inch.

Raj's sister, Soraya, came to tell Raj that lunch was ready. She was carrying her radio. The radio was playing pop music — full blast.

Soraya leaned toward the basket to admire Ramjam. The snake opened both eyes. Then he curled gracefully upward, and flicked his tongue with pleasure.

Soraya laughed. "So much for your flute playing, Raj! Ramjam's like me. He prefers pop music!"

**I**t was Nancy's first day at school. She didn't want to go at all.

"You'll enjoy it when you get there, darling," said her mother, helping her on with her new jacket.

"No, I won't," said Nancy, a tear rolling down her furry cheek. "I'd much rather stay at home with you."

The school was a small red building with flowers growing all around it. And there were pictures hanging in all the windows.

Sadly, Nancy watched her mother walk away. Now she was all alone with strangers. Mrs. Loppity the teacher led her into the schoolroom and introduced her to the other bunnies. Nancy sat beside a rabbit called Ruth. First they drew a picture. Then they went outside to play in the sandbox. Then they played hide-and-seek. After lunch Mrs. Loppity read them an exciting story about a pirate. Then they sang a song and did some dancing. It seemed hardly any time at all before Nancy's mother came to get her.

"I've had such a wonderful time," Nancy said. "Can I come again tomorrow?"

**M**other Rabbit had promised to take Tom and Joe to the fairground, but it was pouring with rain.

"I'm sorry," she said, "but we can't go now."

"Oh, no," groaned the two little bunnies. "We've got nothing to do now."

"Why don't you make your own fairground right here at home?" said Mother Rabbit. "I'll give you some raisins and some popcorn for prizes."

"Great!" said Joe and Tom.

First, they made a big slide with the mattress from Tom's bed. Then they made a lucky numbers game, where every number was lucky and you always got a prize. Then they made a game where you throw rings over the prizes, and you could have as many throws as you wanted.

When Mother Rabbit came to tell them to get ready for bed, Tom and Joe were still playing.

"We've been to the best fairground ever," they said. "You get hundreds of turns on everything, and you win a prize every time!"

**T**ears ran down Susan Rabbit's furry cheeks. Today she was getting married — but a greedy moth had got into her closet and found her wedding dress.

"I can't possibly walk down the aisle in a dress full of holes!" she said to her bridesmaids. "What can I do?"

They thought and thought. Suddenly, Susan had an idea. Soon they were all scampering around the countryside picking white wild flowers — white campion and wood anemone, cloudberry and dewberry, Star of Bethlehem and stitchwort, bindweed and cuckoo flower, mayweed and ox-eye daisy. Then they stitched them all together with gossamer.

What a magnificent wedding dress! It was *far* prettier than the original one! And what a beautiful bride Susan made, dressed ear-to-toe in white flowers!

As Susan walked into the church, the whole congregation gasped — including a very tubby, red-faced moth, hiding in the rafters!

**M**r. and Mrs. Rabbit, Josh, and Baby Rabbit were going on a picnic. Mrs. Rabbit carried the picnic things, Mr. Rabbit carried Baby Rabbit, and Josh ran on in front.

At last, they came to a clearing. There was a stretch of green grass, and some logs to sit on.

"This looks like a good place for a picnic," said Mrs. Rabbit.

"Oh, no," said Mr. Rabbit. "Let's go a bit farther. I'm sure there's a better place farther on."

They walked, and walked, and walked.

"Are we nearly there?" asked Josh, who was getting hungry.

"Nearly there," said Mr. Rabbit, and he marched on.

Soon, Baby Rabbit began to cry.

"Are we nearly there? asked Josh, again.

"In a minute," replied Mr. rabbit.

Eventually, even Mr. Rabbit felt tired. "Here we are!" he said. "Now we can have our picnic lunch."

"It's much too late to have lunch," said Josh, looking at his watch. "We'll have to have a picnic *supper* instead!"

**L**ola had lost her favorite marble. She couldn't find it anywhere. She had emptied out all the drawers and rummaged through all the cupboards in her room. Now the room was in a terrible mess.

"Tidy up your room, this minute!" ordered Lola's mother. "And if you tidy it properly, I'll help you find your marble."

It took Lola a long time to tidy her room. At last she called, "Finished!"

"Good," said her mother. "I'll help you now. Maybe your marble is in the kitchen."

They pulled out the kitchen table. No marble. All they found was Father Rabbit's comb.

They pulled out the chairs. No marble. All they found was Father Rabbit's screwdriver.

They pulled out the oven. No marble. All they found was Father Rabbit's lost wallet.

"I wish I could find my marble," sighed Lola.

"Never mind," said her mother. "At least your father will be pleased, now we've found all his things."

And he was. He was so pleased, he went straight to the toy store and bought Lola three huge, shiny, beautiful new marbles!

# D

oc Dentist lived on a small island in the middle of a lake. In the lake lived a huge monster, called Scarawat. He spent most of his time asleep. And if anything ever woke him up he would lash his tail, blow bubbles, and make terrible waves.

Once a week Doc Dentist had to row across the lake. He always tried to row quietly, so as not to wake Scarawat. But Scarawat had very keen ears and the rabbit's rowing always woke him up. Then Scarawat would make such huge waves with his tail that Doc Dentist's boat would turn right over, and he would end up in the lake.

One day, Doc Dentist was rowing across the lake when he caught sight of Scarawat. Scarawat was holding his jaw, lashing his tail, and groaning terribly. He had toothache!

The brave rabbit swam into Scarawat's mouth and pulled out his aching tooth.

Now, whenever Scarawat wakes up, he just wags his tail and makes gentle waves. And Doc Dentist never, ever, gets wet.

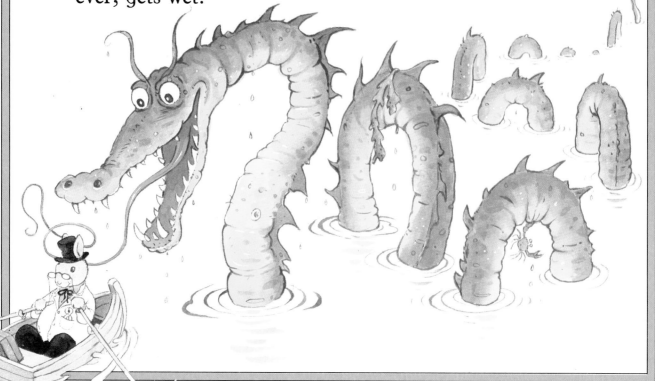

**A** rabbit's life can be hard. Rabbits have many enemies — the fox, the weasel, the racoon, the owl — and because they have such large families it is not always easy to find enough food. But none had had a harder life than old Fred Rabbit.

Lighting his pipe in his armchair by the fire, his audience sitting at his feet, he would begin. "When I was living in the wild, rugged mountains, the biggest, meanest, ugliest bear you've ever seen came so close I could feel his hot breath on my face. 'I'm going to eat you for my supper,' it growled. 'You'll have to catch me first,' I said, and ran as fast as I could, the old bear lumbering and rumbling behind me. Now bears' brakes are none too good, so I led him straight into the deepest, darkest river I knew and swerved at the last minute. He went splashing in, straight into the jaws of a crocodile. So I lived to see another day."

Old Fred sucked on his pipe. The young rabbits' eyes shone. My, how brave old Fred was. They believed every word. Don't you?

lice was always getting lost. One beautiful spring day, she went for a long, long walk. Of course she got hopelessly lost, but she sensibly marked the tree trunks with chalk marks so she would find her way home. Eventually, she ended up in some sand dunes by the sea. She had never seen the sea before!

She returned to the warren to find an urgent meeting in progress. "Alice, we've got to find somewhere else to live," the rabbits told her. "A fox family have moved into the forest. They have already frightened two of our babies."

"I know just the place!" she cried, and told them about the sand dunes.

"But Alice — how will you find them again?" they asked.

Alice told them about the chalk marks she had made.

So that night the rabbits moved lock, stock and barrel to the sand dunes. It was a very roundabout route because Alice kept losing the chalk marks, but they got there eventually. They named the new warren "Alice's Place." They all loved living beside the sea, far away from the foxes!

"See, if I hadn't got lost we'd never have got here," Alice laughed.

**L**et's go to the Moon," said Sandy to Billy. "We'll need helmets and a spaceship."

"And a moon buggy and some boots," said Billy.

They put on their rubber boots and got two pots from the kitchen for helmets.

Sandy and Billy set out two chairs in the bedroom.

"Climb up," shouted Billy. "This is our spaceship. 10 — 9 — 8 — 7 — 6 — 5 — 4 — 3 — 2 — 1 — We have lift-off!"

"There's the Moon," yelled Sandy. "Look out, we're going to crash!"

The two bunnies jumped onto their beds, and landed on the Moon. Crash!

"Oh, no!" screamed Billy. "There's a meteorite. Dive for cover!" And they scrambled under the bedclothes.

When their mother came upstairs, Sandy and Billy were still under the bedclothes.

"Good boys!" she said. "I was going to tell you to get ready for bed. But you've already done it!"

**M**r. Sidney Rabbit was very regular in his habits. Every morning he would put on a pinstripe suit, blue striped shirt and plain blue tie. He would kiss his wife goodbye, catch the 8:16 train, arrive in the office at 8:55 and say "Good morning," to his colleagues. For lunch he always ate a carrot sandwich and an apple that he had brought with him in his briefcase. At one minute to five he would leave the office to catch the 5:17 train home. "You can set your watch by Mr. Sidney Rabbit," his colleagues joked.

Then one day, things went very wrong. Sidney didn't arrive in the office till 9:15, and he was wearing a yellow tie! He clean forgot to say "Good morning," there was no carrot sandwich at lunchtime, and he left the office at 4:30! The next day he also arrived late, and this time he *wasn't wearing a tie at all*!

His colleagues were very worried about him. What could be wrong with Mr. Sidney Rabbit? What had happened?

The next day all was revealed, because at lunchtime the office door opened, and there stood his wife with five tiny, beautiful babies. Sidney had become a father!

**G**ipsy Rose Rabbit was in trouble. She made her living by telling fortunes, but she had lost her crystal ball.

How could she look deep and mysterious without a crystal ball?

Gipsy Rose searched all over her house. She looked under the table, under the bed, and behind the curtains.

It was no good. She would *have* to go to her magic mirror.

> "Mirror, mirror on the wall,
> Where, oh where's my crystal ball?"

There was no reply from the mirror. Just Gipsy Rose's pretty face smiling back at her.

Gipsy Rose began to get hungry. "I've spent so long searching for my ball," she said, "it must be supper time. I'll just check."

Gipsy Rose went outside to find a dandelion clock.

What a relief! There, among the dandelions, was the missing crystal ball.

"It's a bit murky," thought Gipsy Rose. But when she looked closely at her crystal ball she could see her future clearly — lettuce for supper!

**O**nce, there was a king rabbit who was very vain. He was always looking in the mirror and worrying about his clothes.

The king loved swimming, but he thought he looked silly in his striped bathing suit. So whenever he went swimming, he commanded that no one should come anywhere near the lake.

One day, while he was swimming, two robbers crept up and stole his fine clothes and his crown. When the king came out of the lake he found he had no clothes to put on!

An old rabbit, who had been gathering firewood, happened to be wandering near the lake.

"Stop! Stop!" the king commanded. "I'm the king. Give me your clothes. No one must see me in my bathing suit."

"You're not the king," laughed the old rabbit. "The king always wears fancy clothes, and he has a crown." And he ran off laughing, leaving the king in his bathing suit.

The vain king realized how silly he had been. And from then on, he invited all the rabbits in the kingdom to come and swim with him whenever they wished. And he always wore his striped bathing suit!

**J**oy Rabbit wanted a friend. So she went to the farmyard.

The first animal she met was a hen. "Hello," said Joy. "Doing anything? Can I be your friend?"

"I'm laying an egg," snapped the hen. "I only want a friend I can lay eggs with."

The next animal Joy met was a cow. "Hello," said Joy. "Doing anything? Can I be your friend?"

"I'm being milked," yawned the cow. "I only want a friend who can talk about the cream I've made."

The third animal Joy met was a goat. "Doing anything?" said Joy. "Can I be your friend?"

"I'm eating this and that," munched the goat. "I want a friend who can eat everything in sight. It helps keep the farmyard tidy."

Then, finally, Joy met a sheep. "Doing anything?" asked Joy. "Can I be your friend?"

"I'm just thinking," said the sheep. "But it would be more fun to have someone to think with. I'd like you to be my friend!"

**S**am Bunny was bored.

"I know what to do," he thought. "I'll decorate my bedroom."

So, Sam brought out his brushes and some bright orange paint. The can of paint was very hard to open. Sam pushed and pulled and prodded the lid with all his strength. Then, suddenly — whoosh! — the lid flew off, and the paint spattered out in all directions.

Sam looked around his bedroom. His carpet was covered in orange paint, his bed was covered in orange paint, his slippers were covered in orange paint. And when he looked in the mirror he saw that he, too, was covered from head to toe in orange paint!

It took Sam all afternoon to get his room clean, and he had to take three baths himself.

"That's enough decorating for today," thought Sam. "And next time, I think I'll choose another color. *Any* color but orange!"

**L**et's play princes and princesses," said George to Cindy. "You can be a princess, and I'll rescue you. I'm the bravest prince in the world."

"I want to be a prince, too," said Cindy.

"You can't be," said George. "You're a girl. And I'm going to rescue you."

"I don't want to be a princess, and I don't want to be rescued," said Cindy.

George put some chairs around Cindy. "A wicked giant has put you in this cage," he said, "and now I'm going to rescue you."

Cindy began to cry. "I don't want to be in a cage," she wailed.

Mrs. Rabbit came into the room. "What's the matter?" she said.

"I want to be a brave prince," said Cindy.

"And I want to rescue somebody," said George.

"I have an idea" said Mrs. Rabbit. "The terrible giant can put me in his cage, and both of you can rescue me."

"I'm coming," shouted George. "I'm the bravest prince in the world."

Cindy ran after him. "Wait for me," she shouted, "because I'm the bravest *princess* in the world — and I'm coming too!"

**F**rank was off to the zoo. Even though he knew he wasn't supposed to feed the animals, he had saved his best carrot to give to one of them.

First, he went to see the monkeys. He poked his carrot into their cage.

"That doesn't look like a banana," said the monkeys, and they carried on swinging from branch to branch.

Next, Frank went to see the lions. He dangled his carrot through the bars.

"That doesn't look like a steak," said the lions, and they yawned and stretched out in the sun.

Then Frank went to see the elephants. He waved his carrot at them.

"That doesn't look like a bun," said the elephants, looking down their trunks at Frank.

"I want to see the kangaroos," said Frank. He hopped up to the kangaroo cage with his carrot.

Katie Kangaroo was rather short-sighted. "That looks just like a baby to me," she said, and scooped Frank through the bars and put him into her pouch.

Luckily, the zookeeper soon came and rescued Frank. But Frank decided from then on he would do what he was told, and never, ever, feed the animals!

**B**arney loved telling jokes. If he could have had his way he would have spent all day telling them. The trouble was, his family had heard them so many times they were absolutely sick of them.

He wished he could meet someone new who hadn't heard his jokes.

One night, Barney and his brothers and sisters were tucked up snugly in bed. Little did they know that a ginger-colored stranger was slinking down the sandy passage toward their bedroom.

"Who goes there?" Barney squeaked.

"It is I, Peregrine Weasel," said the weasel. "I've come to eat you up."

The rabbits shook in their beds, and the younger ones started to cry.

"Er, before you do, perhaps you could let me to tell you a couple of jokes," said Barney, clearing his throat.

"All right," said the weasel. "Just as long as they make me laugh."

So Barney told the weasel every joke he knew. The weasel laughed so much he completely forgot the reason for his visit, and went off chuckling to himself.

"See, my jokes have saved your lives," said Barney. And from then on, no one ever moaned about Barney's jokes ever again.

**W**ho turns the stars on at night?" asked Little Rabbit.

"Nobody turns the stars on," said Father Rabbit. "They're there all the time. We just don't see them in the daytime."

In the middle of the night, Little Rabbit woke up. "I wonder if the stars are shining?" he thought.

He ran to the window and looked out. The sky was full of clouds. All the stars were hidden.

"The stars have all gone out," cried Little Rabbit. "Someone's turned the stars off!"

Father Rabbit came upstairs. "Don't worry," he said to Little Rabbit. "The clouds are hiding the stars. The stars are still shining."

He switched on Little Rabbit's flashlight and put it under the bedclothes. "Look," he said, "you can't see the light now, can you? But it's still shining. It's the same with the stars."

"When will the stars run out?" asked Little Rabbit.

"The stars won't ever run out," Father Rabbit laughed.

"That's good," said Little Rabbit. And, feeling much better, he fell fast asleep.

**A**untie Flo had bought Ron and Debby a water pistol each. They were the best water pistols Ron and Debby had ever seen, and they couldn't wait to try them out.

"Let's wait until it's night time," said Ron. "Then we can go and hunt for burglars and shoot them with our water pistols."

In the middle of the night Debby woke Ron up. "Wake up," she said. "I can hear a burglar in the kitchen. Let's go catch him."

The two rabbits grabbed their water pistols and crept into the kitchen. The kitchen was very still and quiet. There were strange shadows all around, and the owls were hooting outside.

Suddenly, they heard footsteps. "Help! Burglars!" cried Debby.

Then the lights went on. There, in the kitchen, stood Father Rabbit. "Don't shoot!" he laughed. "It's only me. I only came to get a glass of milk!"

**A**s you probably know, rabbits have very large families. But none was as large as Patricia's. Her burrow was overrun with noisy little bunnies. They slept six to a bed, their washing filled ten clothes lines — but it was all that cooking that really got her down.

One day, Patricia had only just finished cooking breakfast when Benny, her youngest son, was asking her what was for lunch.

"You'll have to get your own today," she announced. "I'm off for a walk, and I might be gone quite a long time."

How peaceful the countryside seemed after the noisy burrow. She could actually hear herself think! She walked across a cornfield and sat beneath a shady oak tree. But gradually, she began to feel a little lonely. And so she went home.

"We've missed you so much, Mommy," said her children, jumping all over her.

"And I've missed you too, my darlings," cried Patricia, kissing each in turn.

That night they ate lettuce soup and carrot cake — Patricia's favorites — made not by her, but by her children. And they promised that, from then on, they'd take turns to cook a meal everyday!

**H**umphrey had hiccups. Whatever he did, whatever he tried to say, he hiccuped.

"Hold your breath!" said Grandmother.

"Hic!" said Humphrey.

"Pull yourself together!" said Father.

"Hic!" said Humphrey.

"Sip some lemonade," said Uncle Bill.

"Hic!" said Humphrey.

"Drink a glass of water upside down!" said Cousin Pete.

"Hic!" said Humphrey.

"Go and play with your puppy," said Mother.

Humphrey sat bolt upright with surprise. Grandmother, Father, Uncle Bill, Cousin Pete, and Mother all held their breath.

"What puppy? I don't have a puppy," cried Humphrey.

Humphrey's mother smiled. "We bought you a puppy, for doing well at school. Now you've stopped hiccuping, I'll bring him in."

# THE PICTURE

**I**'m going to paint a picture today," said Skip.

"What are you going to paint?" asked Tim.

"I don't know yet," replied Skip. "I might paint a tree."

So Skip painted a tree. Then, he painted a sun.

"The sun's shining," said Skip.

"Are there any clouds?" asked Tim.

"Not yet," said Skip, "but there will be in a minute."

Skip painted some big grey blotches. The blotches began to drip.

"Now it's raining in your picture," said Skip.

The grey clouds dripped all over the tree.

"I think it's getting dark now," Skip said. "I can't see the tree any more."

Then Skip put black paint over the picture. "It's very dark now," he said. "It's night time. It's black all over. Do you like my picture?"

"It's beautiful!" said Tim. "It's a beautiful picture of a beautiful tree at night time." And he hung it up to dry.

**M**r. Grumbles lived all alone in a damp, untidy cottage. It hadn't seen a duster for years. Dirty dishes were piled to the ceiling, and I don't think I'd better tell you how long it had been since he changed his sheets. "Why should I bother to keep my cottage tidy? I never get any visitors," grumbled Mr. Grumbles.

Mr. Grumbles' birthday was just like any other day. At 11 o'clock he walked to the Rabbit and Carrot tavern, where he drank a glass of elderberry wine.

As he walked back up the lane, grumbling to himself and feeling rather lonely, he heard voices singing *Happy Birthday*. For a moment he wondered whose birthday it was. Then he remembered. It was his! All the villagers were gathered outside his cottage, and as for the cottage itself — it was spick and span! All the dishes had been washed, and there were clean sheets on his bed.

"Well, bless my whiskers!" said Mr. Grumbles to the kind rabbits. "This certainly is a birthday surprise. Perhaps now I might have a few visitors," and for the first time for years he smiled instead of grumbled!

**J**im could never get to sleep.

His parents told him to count sheep, but he kept losing count.

They told him to recite nursery rhymes. Jim shouted them at the top of his voice, but he woke up his brothers and sisters.

His parents called for the doctor. The doctor said Jim would grow out of it in time, but his mother didn't think she could wait that long.

A hypnotist came. Just as he said, "And now you will fall asleep..." Jim woke up.

Finally, Jim's mother went to the library. She took out a book on explorers. She read the adventures to Jim and told him to pretend *he* was an explorer. So Jim did.

One night he was Christopher Columbus, discovering America. Next, he went to darkest Africa — it was so hot in the jungle! Often he was an astronaut, landing on Mars.

Jim had such fun exploring, he soon forgot he couldn't get to sleep. And no one else minded either, because at last there was peace at bedtime!

**B**ecause rabbits have large families, it wasn't very surprising that Mr. and Mrs. Doe had eleven children. What *was* surprising was that they were all girls. Mr. Doe was secretly rather sad about this. He was crazy about soccer and had always dreamt of having his own family team competing in the annual Warren Soccer League. "Just my luck that I have all girls," he smiled.

"Who says girls can't play soccer?" said Elizabeth, his oldest daughter, and whispered something in his furry eat.

The day of the Warren Soccer League Game dawned. Mr. Doe took his place at the edge of the field.

"What bad luck having all daughters," the other fathers said to him. Mr. Doe smiled to himself. Suddenly, everyone's jaws dropped open. For onto the field came the two teams, one of them the Doe family!

The girls didn't win, but they played very well and scored two goals. Mr. Doe swelled with pride. "Next year you're going to win," he beamed. And they did!

**B**etsy and Uncle Bob were at the supermarket. Betsy was carrying her new basket.

"What would you like?" asked the storekeeper.

"Some lettuce, some potatoes, some carrots, and some tomatoes, please," said Uncle Bob.

"And some bananas," said Betsy.

"In a moment," said Uncle Bob. "Next, I'd like some apples, some pears, some oranges, and a cauliflower, please."

"And some bananas," said Betsy.

"And some bananas," said Uncle Bob.

Betsy gave the storekeeper her basket, and the store-keeper put a huge bunch of bananas inside.

Betsy and Uncle Bob picked up their shopping and set off for home. A little way down the road, Betsy stopped. "My basket's so heavy," she groaned.

A little later, she stopped again. "I can't go on any farther," she wailed.

So Uncle Bob had to carry all the shopping, Betsy, Betsy's basket, *and* the bananas all the way home!

# THE MIDNIGHT SECRET

It was midnight. Mrs. Owl and Norman were night animals. They had just eaten their breakfast and were waiting for lunchtime.

Usually the wood was quiet at midnight. But it wasn't quiet that night. There were strange clicking noises, whispering, clattering and giggling sounds.

"What's all that noise?" asked Norman.

There was a loud "shshing" and more giggling.

"What is it?" asked Norman, again.

Then there were different noises: munching, sipping, crunching — and even burping noises!

Just then Mr. Owl came back from hunting.

"Dad," said Norman. "What *are* those noises in the woods?"

Mr. Owl came up close to Norman. "Don't tell anyone, it's meant to be a secret. We're not the only ones awake tonight."

Mr. Owl pointed to the foot of the tree. There, the brown rabbits had spread a blanket. They were having a secret midnight feast.

"I won't tell a soul," whispered Norman to Mr. Owl.

**D**orothy had lost a tooth.

She tried to stick it back with butter, but that didn't work.

She ran her tongue along the space where the tooth had been. "I want my tooth back," she said.

Dorothy kept feeling the space and looking at the gap. By bedtime, she was tired and upset.

"Leave your tooth under your pillow," said her mother. "The Tooth Fairy will come tonight."

"Will she stick my tooth back?" asked Dorothy.

"No," said her father. "You'll grow a new one some day."

Although Dorothy didn't believe in fairies, she put her tooth under the pillow, just in case.

In the morning Dorothy felt better. She even forgot to feel for the gap in her teeth with her tongue.

But then, she remembered to check her pillow . . .

Underneath, where her tooth had been, was a bright new coin! The Tooth Fairy had come after all!

**W**hat are you doing, Jess?" asked Sam.

"I'm making a stew," answered Jess. "It's a witch's stew. You can help me get things for it."

They looked around the garden. Jess found some poppy heads, some marigold seeds, and some bits of lavender. Sam found grass, a dandelion head, and an empty snail shell. Then Jess put them in the bucket and stirred.

"Can I stir too?" asked Sam.

"Yes, but be careful," replied Jess. "It's very strong magic."

"What will the witches do with it?" asked Sam.

"They'll drink it, of course," said Jess. "But it's not ready yet. Let's get some earth."

The little bunnies scooped up pawfuls of earth, and dropped it in. "I think it's ready now," said Jess.

Sam and Jess hid behind the shed and waited for the witches to come. But then it began to get dark. An owl hooted, the wind whistled. The garden was full of dark shadows.

"Are the witches coming?" asked Sam, who wasn't the least bit frightened.

"Who cares about witches!" said Jess. "I'm going in for supper." And she ran, very quickly, inside!

S tanley was always talking in class. Miss Wainwright would say, "Be quiet, Stanley!" But Stanley just kept on talking.

Whenever Miss Wainwright read to the children, Stanley talked at the same time. Whenever Miss Wainwright wrote on the blackboard, Stanley would chatter to his friends. Whenever Miss Wainwright got out a map of the world, Stanley never even looked up. He'd just go right on talking.

One day, Miss Wainwright decided to do something about it. "We will all study history this morning," she said. "Stanley will come to the front. He can remind us of what we learned last week!"

How could Stanley tell the class what they'd learned last week? He'd been too busy talking.

For the first time ever, Stanley was silent. And then his face turned bright red.

Eventually, Miss Wainwright let him go back to his desk.

After that, Miss Wainwright never had to say, "Be quiet, Stanley!" ever again.

Well, hardly ever!

**I**t was a wet day. As usual, the two bunny sisters were quarreling about what they should play. So Grandpa Bunny decided to tell them a story.

"Long ago," he said, "there were two princess bunnies. They lived in a great castle by the lake. Every day they walked by the lake and looked for beautiful pebbles. And every day they quarreled.

"One day, the ancient god of the lake roared, 'I am tired of your quarreling.' He made a huge whirlwind, which sucked all the pebbles to the bottom of the lake.

"'Oh,' wailed the princesses. 'Our pebbles have gone.'

"After many months of searching, they found one pebble lying on the shore.

"'You have it, sister,' said one.

"'No, you have it,' said the other.

"The god of the lake was pleased, and he brought all the pebbles back to the shore again."

When Grandpa Bunny's story was over, the two bunny sisters jumped up. "Let's play princesses," said one.

"Oh, yes," said the other. And they ran off to build a castle together.

**S**ally Rabbit was very untidy. On the day she was going on vacation, she left her packing till the last minute. Eventually, she managed to find her swim suit under her bed and her sunglasses at the back of the kitchen drawer, but *where was her passport?*

"I'm sure I put it here," she said, opening up a cupboard. But, no passport.

"Or perhaps here," she said, emptying every drawer in her desk. But, no passport. "Oh dear, I'm going to miss the airplane," she cried, frantically searching high and low. "How I *wish* I was tidy."

At last she found the passport — at the bottom of the laundry basket.

But it was too late. The plane had flown without her.

So Sally spent her vacation not sunbathing on the beach, but at home tidying her house. My, how tidy it looked! "And that's the way it's going to stay," she told herself firmly.

Sally never missed the plane again, because from then on her passport was always kept in its proper place — in a file called "Passport!"

**L**ittle Bo was the smallest rabbit in the warren. He couldn't run as fast as the other rabbits; he couldn't thump as loudly when there was danger.

One year, the rain stopped coming. It had not rained for weeks and weeks. The grass turned brown, and the rabbits were hungry.

Three of the biggest, strongest rabbits went off to find fresh food. Little Bo wanted to go with them, but they laughed at him. "You're far too small to come with us," they said.

Four days later, the rabbits returned. They had found nothing but dry, empty deserts and rocks.

Little Bo decided to set off on his own. "I'll follow the dried-up river," he thought.

He followed the dried-up river far into the hills. At last, high up on a hillside, he found a trickle of water. And beside the water lay fields of fresh grass — enough to feed all the rabbits until the rain came again.

After that, Little Bo was given a new name. They called him The Great Finder.

**D**ebbie had been sent outside because she wanted to play her harmonica. "Don't make that *awful noise* in here," her mother had said.

Debbie wandered off. It began to grow foggy. Her mother looked out at the mist. She wanted Debbie safely inside.

Debbie's mother searched outside.

She looked in the wood shed.

She looked by the stream.

She looked in Debbie's little tree house.

It was difficult to find her way in the fog. And Debbie was nowhere to be seen. Debbie's mother was beginning to get very worried.

Then she heard a faint sound. What was it? Of course! It was Debbie's harmonica.

Debbie's mother followed the noise. It grew louder and louder. At last she found Debbie. She was hidden behind the holly bush.

Debbie's mother smiled and hugged her.

"I *am* pleased to see you," she said. "And for the first time ever I was pleased to hear *that awful noise!*"

**S**wift Foot and White Toe had just arrived at the ocean. They couldn't wait to go to the beach and see the sea.

"All right little bunnies, you may go," said their mother. "But remember, beware of the Tide."

The two little bunnies ran toward the beach.

"What is the Tide?" White Toe asked his sister.

Just then, a large black gull swooped down. The rabbits crouched low. "Perhaps that is the Tide," said Swift Foot.

At last they reached the beach, and they ran towards the sea.

A large crab scuttled past White Toe. "Perhaps that is the Tide," he said, jumping out of its way.

The bunnies played for a long time. Then they climbed on to a sandbank and fell asleep.

When the rabbits woke up, there was water all around them.

"Oh, no," cried White Toe. "The sand has disappeared."

"Let's go," cried Swift Foot, "before somebody thinks we've stolen it."

"We went to sleep and the sand disappeared," cried the rabbits, when they had reached home.

"I told you to beware of the Tide, didn't I?" laughed their mother.

Tommy had measles. He lay in bed and groaned.

"Try not to scratch," said his mother. "We'll do a jigsaw puzzle together."

Then Tommy's sister came to see him. "I'll read to you," she said.

Before Tommy went to sleep, Daddy sat on the end of his bed. They had a long talk about camping and fishing.

The next day, two friends came to visit. They brought Tommy some paints.

Aunt Olivia baked him a cake. Grandma Gertrude brought some soda pop.

The time went quickly. So did Tommy's spots.

One night Tommy's mother put out his school clothes. When she came back to tuck him in, she got a shock. Tommy was covered in spots again.

Then she saw the paintbox. Tommy didn't want the fun to end. He had made some new spots all of his own!

**W**endy Rabbit wanted a photograph of her family, so she sent for Froggy the photographer.

Wendy's family lined up, dressed in their best clothes. Froggy dived under his black cloth and looked through the lens of his camera. "Say 'Carrots,'" he said.

Mr. and Mrs. Rabbit, Wendy, Henry, and Linda were all smiling. But little Sidney had hidden his face behind his paws.

Froggy sang a song, but Sidney stayed behind his paws.

Froggy told a joke; Sidney hid behind his paws.

Froggy made his bow tie spin round. Still, Sidney hid behind his paws.

"I know," thought Froggy. "I'll stand on my head."

Froggy just about managed it, but then . . . he split his pants — *RIP!*

When Sidney heard that, he peeked from behind his paws — and laughed and laughed.

Froggy rushed to his camera. Snap! He took a lovely photograph.

And later, Mrs. Rabbit sewed up his pants.

Late one summer's evening there was a terrible thunderstorm. The air was hot and heavy, and large drops of rain began hurtling to the ground. One by one, all the rabbits stopped feeding and ran to their burrows on the steep, sandy bank.

Little Thumper was the last of the rabbits to take shelter. She sat watching the river as the rain lashed and churned the water, the lightning flashed in the sky, and the thunder shook the trees. At last, very wet, she too ran into the burrow.

The other rabbits were soon asleep, but Little Thumper could not sleep at all. After a time she climbed out of the burrow again.

The night was very dark. Little Thumper felt the rain on her nose, and heard the dreadful roar of the river. Then, suddenly, there was another flash of lightning, and in the terrible flash Little Thumper saw that the river had flooded over the river bank. The grey water was rising toward the rabbits' burrow.

Little Thumper ran back to warn the other rabbits. They all managed to scramble from their burrows and race up the hill before the swirling waters reached their holes. Little Thumper had saved them all!

O ne morning, the rabbits awoke to find the world covered in a thick white carpet of snow. All the little bunnies put on their hats and coats and gloves and rushed out to play. First they had a snowball fight, then they built a snow rabbit, then they went tobogganing. What fun it all was.

"Come and look," cried Andrea suddenly, for she had spotted in the snow some strange, large, oval-shaped footprints.

The rabbits gathered round. What kind of animal could have such huge feet?

"Perhaps it's a bull," said Jimmy.

"Or a very large . . . fox," whispered Suzy.

"There's only one way to find out," said Andrea. "We'll follow the tracks."

So they did, Andrea bravely leading the way. The tracks led them across the heath and into Shady Wood. It was very dark and silent and cold, and the rabbits began to tremble. What if it turned out to be, say, a *wolf*?

Suddenly, the footprints ended. And there, collecting wood for his fire, was old Noah Rabbit — wearing large snow shoes! How they all laughed!

**H**oneybun was planning her future. "What should I be when I'm a grown-up rabbit?" she thought.

"Should I be a ballerina? I could dance all over the world.

"Should I be a hairdresser? I could make rabbits beautiful and dye their fur.

"Should I be a detective? I could wear an old raincoat and hunt for clues.

"Should I be a musician? I could play the flute, or even the harp.

"Should I be an ice cream seller? I could drive a van, and eat up all the leftovers.

"Should I be a doctor? I could wear a white coat and make my patients better.

"Should I be a film star? I could smile at my fans and sign autographs.

"Should I be a teacher? I could say, 'Be quiet, children! Listen to me!'"

Suddenly, Honeybun caught sight of the clock. It was almost 8:30.

"Should I eat my breakfast and go to school?" she said. "Yes, perhaps, for now I should just do that!"

**L**ong, long ago, in a small village, there lived a rabbit magician, called Silver Ears. He only ever made good magic, and his powers were astonishing.

The king heard what Silver Ears could do. He sent for him and commanded him to make some gold.

"I can't do that," said Silver Ears. "Gold will make you greedy, and that would not be a good thing."

The king was angry, and ordered Silver Ears to be thrown into a cage. But Silver Ears's magic was so powerful, he made the bars of the cage crumble.

Then the king ordered his guards to put Silver Ears in chains. But the chains slipped easily from his paws.

The king was so angry at this, he stamped his foot hard on the floor. His foot made a great hole, and he fell down it — straight into a pile of hay! And the good magician, Silver Ears, went home to his small village, laughing all the way.

# COOKING LESSONS

The Bunny-Smiths were learning to cook. Their teacher, Walter, had once been a chef in a fancy hotel.

Walter taught the Bunny-Smiths to make carrot stew. Henry spilt most of his on the floor. But Walter didn't mind, even when he slipped on it.

Walter showed them how to toss pancakes. Dotty's pancake was sticky, like glue. But Walter didn't mind, even when it got stuck to the ceiling.

Then they prepared some salad. Walter didn't mind when Lucy screamed and screamed, "I'VE GOT A SLUG IN MY LETTUCE!"

Next, he showed them how to cook spaghetti. Henry's and Dotty's and Lucy's was delicious. But Freddy didn't concentrate. He got spaghetti on his paws, spaghetti around his ears, and spaghetti up his nose.

"Ugh, this is TOO MUCH, even for me," cried Walter. "You can all go home early — for a bath!"

B renda had lost her blanket. It wasn't in her bed; it wasn't in the bathroom; it wasn't by her favorite chair.

Brenda stopped to think. She sucked her thumb. But her thumb didn't taste right; not without her blanket.

"Why don't you go out and play?" said Brenda's father.

"I can't," said Brenda. "I've lost my blanket."

"Never mind," said her father. "Tomorrow, we're going away to the beach."

Two big tears rolled down Brenda's cheeks. She didn't want to go to the beach. Not without her blanket.

Brenda didn't want anyone to see her cry, so she hopped outside into the back yard.

In the yard, Brenda's mother was hanging out the washing.

What a long line of washing it was! There were all the clothes, washed and ready for the holiday: teeshirts, sundresses, swim suits, towels, little white socks, and right at the end . . . Brenda's blanket!

**I**t was winter. The little bunny had explored all the fields near his burrow, and it was getting hard to find fresh food to eat.

One day the bunny wandered farther than usual and came to the edge of the wood. There, he saw a large hole in the foot of an oak tree.

Just then, a large shadow swooped overhead. It was a barn owl! The little bunny dived into the hole to escape.

He sat quite still for a moment. Suddenly, he felt something land on his head. Bonk! Then another, and another. "Ouch!" he cried.

"Who's stealing my acorns?" came a voice from above.

"Not me," said the little bunny.

"Good!" said the voice. It was a squirrel, and now he had scampered down the tree and was peering at the bunny. "What are you doing there?" he asked. "I thought you were after my food."

"I thought *you* were a barn owl," said the bunny. "I think I'd better find another hole. Goodbye."

And the little bunny scampered off home.

Tex was an ordinary little rabbit. But he liked to talk big.

When his friends rode their bikes, Tex said, "My bike goes a hundred miles an hour."

If he was asked to play football, Tex said, "I scored fifty touchdowns last week."

When he wrote a story at school, his favorite words were MILLIONS and ZILLIONS.

Tex's teacher spoke to his mother. "Leave things to me," Tex's mother said.

The next day Tex was late getting home. "I'm starving," he said. "I could eat fifty sandwiches."

Tex's mother didn't say a word. She just brought in a large plate. On it were fifty sandwiches.

Tex tried not to look surprised. After ten sandwiches he began to feel ill. "I'm dying," he groaned.

Then Tex thought carefully. "Well, I'm not exactly dying," he said. "I'm just full. I guess I asked for *too many* sandwiches!"

I'm going exploring," said Alice.

"But you can't go now," said her mother. "It's raining."

"Explorers don't mind the rain," said Alice, and she went outside.

It had been raining for quite a long time. There was a huge puddle in the back yard.

"First," said Alice, "I have to cross this terrible river. I must watch out for crocodiles!"

When she'd reached the other side safely, she took out her telescope. There was a large patch of nettles on the grass.

"That looks like a terrible jungle," said Alice. She picked up a stick and began to beat through the nettles. Ouch! The nettles stung her legs and hands, and she ran back inside the house.

"There are terrible stinging plants in the jungle," Alice cried.

"Never mind," said her mother. "I'll rub it better for you. Have you finished exploring now?"

"Yes," said Alice. "I certainly have!"

# SHIRLEY AND SHEILA

It was spring time, and Shirley had a new friend. She was called Sheila. Sheila was a caterpillar.

Shirley and Sheila had a lot in common. They enjoyed lying in the sunshine. They were fond of a gentle walk. They liked reading together.

One day Sheila wasn't at their meeting place. Shirley was sad and lonely. After days and days of looking for Sheila she began to give up hope.

Suddenly she saw a bright flash of color dancing past her eyes.

"Hello," said a cheerful voice.

Shirley recognized the voice, but she couldn't believe her eyes. Sheila had turned into a beautiful butterfly.

"Follow me," cried Sheila, flying off around the fields. "We'll make up for lost time."

"Slow down," replied Shirley. "I don't know if I can keep up with you now."

And the two friends raced happily into the sunshine.

**E**veryone was frightened of old Mrs. Williams. She wore a pointed black hat and a long black dress. Rumor had it that she was a witch and that if you went near her you would have bad luck for a year. All the rabbits kept a long way away from her.

One day, Mrs. Williams was out shopping when she dropped her parcels. Some boys were playing nearby, but only Joseph helped her pick them up.

"You'll have bad luck for a year, Joseph," the others joked, and ran away.

The next morning, a gleaming red bicycle mysteriously appeared outside Joseph's house. It had "Joseph" painted on the crossbar. It could have only come from one person — Mrs. Williams!

"She must be a *good* witch, not a bad one," said Joseph.

After that, his friends began to follow old Mrs. Williams around in the hope she would drop her parcels again. But she never did!

**J**oe and Jessie had just finished breakfast.

"What do you want to do today?" asked their mother.

Jessie sighed, "I don't know."

Joe sighed, "I don't know either."

"Well," said their mother, "you'd better have a think."

Joe and Jessie sat and thought.

"I can't think of anything," said Joe.

Jessie looked up. "I've thought of something," she said.

Jessie sat on a chair and looked very hard at the floor.

"Please tell me what you're doing," begged Joe.

"I can't," said Jessie. "It's a secret."

Joe stood and watched her. He hopped from one foot to the other. "Humph!" he said. "This secret's very boring."

Then he climbed on a chair next to Jessie and looked down at the floor too.

After a while, their mother came in. "What are you two doing?" she asked.

"It's a secret," they both replied.

But do you know what was the biggest secret of all? No one, not even Jessie, knew what the secret was!

**H**eather had been to the fair. She had won a huge red balloon.

"Hold the balloon tightly," warned her parents.

As Heather skipped along she tripped on a fallen branch and let go of the string. The balloon floated right to the top of a tree.

"My red balloon! My red balloon!" wailed Heather.

"We told you so," said her parents.

"What's all the noise about?" grumbled a voice from the tree.

It was Barney Owl. The balloon had landed on his perch and woken him up.

"Please, can I have my balloon back?" asked Heather. "I won it at the fair."

"The fair? The fair?" gasped Barney. "Ooh, toowit, twooh, I've overslept."

He flew down carefully with the balloon.

"Hold tight, Heather," said Barney, giving it back to her. "I'm off to the fair. Maybe I can win a balloon too."

**R**omeo Rabbit was very vain. He was always looking in the mirror. "Don't be so vain," said his mother. "It's what's inside that counts."

Romeo took no notice. He spent all his money on a new red coat. He wanted to show off his coat, so he went for a walk in the field.

In the field was a bull. And when the bull saw Romeo's red coat, he charged at Romeo and tossed him out of the field and into the farmyard. Squelch! Romeo landed in the pig sty.

"Nice jacket," said the pig.

Romeo burst into tears. He cried all the way home. He smelled awful.

His mother ran him a bath. Then Romeo wrapped himself in a towel. He didn't want to look in the mirror. He wanted his mother to comfort him.

Romeo's mother smiled. "Never mind," she said. "I don't care how you look. It's what's inside that counts!" And she gave him a great big hug.

**T**wo baby rabbits were sitting on the river bank, nibbling the long grass. It was so quiet by the river. They watched the baby ducks bobbing up and down in the water.

"I wish we could swim," said one baby rabbit.

"Yes, so do I," said the other.

They watched some little chicks walking on a raft made of floating logs.

"Look!" said the first baby rabbit. "I bet we could do that. You go first."

"No, you go first," said the other.

"Let's jump together," they both agreed.

The logs were floating close to the river bank. With a short run and a hop, both rabbits landed on a log.

The logs began to sink, and both rabbits tumbled into the water. "Ugh! Help! Splutter!" they cried.

The water was not deep, and both rabbits managed to clamber to the shore. They shook the water from their ears, and then they sat quietly in the sun and waited for their fur to dry.

"I like it here on the grass best," said the first rabbit.

"Yes," agreed the second, "so do I."

**R**ichard Rabbit was a terrible snorer. My, how he snored! He kept all the other rabbits awake. Eventually they banished him to a burrow right on the edge of the warren, so he wouldn't disturb anyone.

One night, while Richard was snoring to his heart's content, a greedy fox crept up. He could smell rabbit — and he was hungry! Suddenly, he paused and pricked up his ears. What on earth was that noise? It sounded like the growl of a very ferocious animal! What could it be? A bear? A lion? A tiger? The fox didn't wait to find out. He turned around and ran off into the night.

So it was all thanks to Richard's snoring that the rabbits slept safe in their beds that night!

**M**rs. Gray was lying in bed. It was Sunday. She didn't want to get up. She wanted to snooze.

"Just ten minutes more," she said to herself. "Then I must make breakfast." She tried not to think about next week's meals. Her last thought was, "I wonder how young rabbits manage to eat so much?"

Mrs. Gray woke with a start. It felt very late. She dressed quickly and ran downstairs. Why weren't the Gray Rabbits shouting for their breakfast?

At the bottom of the stairs six bunnies rushed forward. Mr. Gray beamed behind them. They all shouted at once.

But they weren't shouting for their breakfast. They were shouting "HAPPY MOTHER'S DAY."

What a lovely surprise! The Gray Rabbits had been up since dawn. They had filled the house with flowers and had hung up their cards. And best of all — they had cooked a huge Mother's Day breakfast!

**E**ach year the rabbits played tug of war against the squirrels. The squirrels always won. But they cheated. They got their friends to throw nuts at the rabbits to distract them. So the rabbits made a plan.

The teams lined up. The squirrels flexed their muscles. "This is going to be easy," they said.

The rabbits and the squirrels pulled as hard as they could.

"NOW!" shouted the rabbit at the front.

The rabbits let go of the rope suddenly. The squirrels were tugging so hard, they went back, and back, and back... right into the river.

The wet squirrels scuttled back into position. They were furious. They had won the first round, but they didn't dare tug hard again. They were frightened the rabbits would let go and they would end up in the river again.

The rabbits won the competition easily. They hadn't broken the rules. They'd just taught those cheating squirrels a lesson.

**J**ason and Tom's house was on top of a steep hill. One day, it started to snow.

"Let's make a giant snowball," said Tom.

The two bunnies gathered some snow together and pressed it into a firm ball. Then they rolled it round and round the garden so that it got bigger and bigger.

"Let's take it out into the lane," said Tom. "There's some really deep snow there."

Jason held the gate open, and Tom pushed the snowball. He had just got it onto the lane, when he slipped and let go of it. The snowball began to roll down the hill.

"Oh, you silly!" wailed Jason. "Our snowball's rolling away."

"It wasn't my fault," shouted Tom.

While the two bunnies argued, the snowball carried on rolling down, down, down the hill.

"Quick, let's go after it!" called Jason.

The snowball did not stop rolling until it reached the bottom of the hill.

"Wow!" gasped the little bunnies when they reached the bottom. "Our snowball must be the biggest snowball in the world!"

**W**itch Hazel was having a bad day. She had lost her black cat, and her spells kept going wrong. She couldn't even start her broomstick.

"*Rat-tat-tat!*" Someone was knocking at the door.

Witch Hazel peeked through her curtains. It was Basil Beaver. "Oh, dear, what if he wants a spell?" thought Witch Hazel. "I'm not up to it today."

She decided to hide in the cupboard until Basil went away.

Inside the cupboard Witch Hazel saw two yellow lights piercing the darkness. Then she heard a familiar purring sound.

"Thank goodness!" cried Witch Hazel. "I've found my cat. Everything will be all right now."

She climbed out of the cupboard with her cat, and went to the door.

Basil was still waiting, impatiently. "What kept you?" he asked.

"Er . . . I was just looking for my wand," replied Witch Hazel. Then Witch Hazel did something most unusual for a witch . . . She blushed!

**R**avioli Rabbit was an opera singer. But Ravioli had lost his voice. He took a pill; he sprayed his throat; he gargled, but it was no good. He couldn't say a word.

The concert manager was looking glum. The tickets for tonight's show were all sold out. All the posters outside said, "RAVIOLI'S IN TOWN."

The manager called together the orchestra and singers. "Things look bad," he told them.

Suddenly Ravioli grinned. He wrote a message for the manager. Then the manager grinned too.

"Ravioli is going to change places with the conductor," said the manager. "The conductor knows all the words, and Ravioli will wave his arms and conduct the orchestra."

The show went off without a hitch. Ravioli's fans loved it.

There was only one problem. All that arm waving had given Ravioli a sore back. So now he had a sore back *and* a sore throat!

**B**reakfast's ready," called Toby and Tom's mother. "Hurry up."

Tom was already out of bed and dressed, but little Toby was still under the bedclothes.

Mother Rabbit came upstairs. "What's the matter with Toby?" she said.

She felt Toby's nose. It was very hot. "Perhaps you better have a day in bed," she said.

"What's a day in bed?" asked Toby.

"It means you stay quietly in bed all day and look at books and puzzles," she replied.

Toby had a drink, and then he went back to sleep. When he woke up he asked, "Have I had my day in bed yet?"

"Not yet," replied his mother.

In the afternoon, Tom helped Toby do a jugsaw puzzle, and Mother Rabbit read him a story. Later, she brought him a glass of milk and some cookies. Toby was looking much better.

After supper, Tom came up to get ready for bed. He found Toby sitting on the floor with his clothes on. "What are you doing, Toby?" he said. "It's time to get ready for bed."

"No, it's not," said Toby. "I've had my day in bed. Now I'm getting up!"

**L**eroy was feeling nervous. It was his first night in a tent.

Bud was sharing the tent with Leroy. He'd been camping before.

Suddenly, there was a strange hooting noise.

"What's that?" whispered Leroy.

"It's only an owl," said Bud.

Then, suddenly, there was a bright shaft of light, like lightning.

"What's that?" squealed Leroy.

"It's only the light of the Moon, shining through the tent," said Bud.

Suddenly, something fluttered against Leroy's face.

"What's that?" he gasped. He didn't think he could take much more of this.

"It's just a moth," said Bud. "Try to get some sleep."

The next thing Leroy knew, it was light and there was a strange burning smell.

"FIRE, FIRE," he shouted at the top of his voice.

Bud opened the tent flap. "It's only our sausages cooking for breakfast," he said. "They'll be ready soon."

Leroy jumped up. "YUMMY," he cried. "I think I'm going to like camping."

**H**ow I wish I could fly like that bird," sighed Jack, staring up at one soaring through the sky. "Mind you, if he can do it, perhaps I can too."

He made some wings out of a sheet, climbed into a tree, and jumped. Oww! The ground felt very hard, and he banged his nose.

Next Jack built himself a flying machine out of wood, nails, and rubber bands. He attached himself to it and ran and ran... but his feet remained firmly on the ground. "Oh dear, perhaps rabbits aren't meant to fly after all," he said sadly.

A few days later it was Jack's birthday. And his birthday treat? Yes, a ride in a plane!

How exciting to roar down the runway and take off up into the clouds!

"Rabbits *are* meant to fly, after all!" Jack cried, looking down on the world through the windows. "And I know exactly what I want to be when I grow up. I'm going to be a pilot!"

O zzie Otter puffed along the river bank. He was worn out from trying to teach the bunnies to swim.

The bunnies were such bad pupils. When Ozzie said, "Legs up!" the bunnies put their legs down on the river bed. When Ozzie said, "Tummies flat!" the bunnies curled into a ball and sank like stones. When Ozzie said, "Relax!" the bunnies splashed about in a panic.

Ozzie was beginning to get impatient. "I didn't have this trouble with the frogs," he complained. "I will have to change my tactics."

He called the bunnies over to him. "This is what I want you to do," he said. "Lie back in the water, let your ears touch the surface, then lift your feet up and imagine you are relaxing in your favorite armchair."

Good old Ozzie! The bunnies' big ears acted like water wings. They soon learnt to swim on their backs.

And Ozzie had learnt something too — how to be patient with bunnies!

**L**et's play pirates," said Joe. "We'll sail away in our pirate ship and dig for treasure."

Joe and Scott found two cardboard tubes for telescopes. They turned the garden table upside down for their boat, and found two plastic shovels to row with. Then they climbed aboard.

Joe looked through his telescope. "There's Treasure Island," he shouted, pointing at the flower bed. "Let's dig for treasure."

They leapt off the boat, and began to dig up the flower bed.

"Hey, stop!" shouted their father. "You can't dig there! Dig in the vegetable patch instead."

The two pirates sailed to the vegetable patch, and dug and dug. They found lots of stones, and an old bone, but no treasure.

Later, their father came out holding two shiny coins. "Thanks, pirates," he said. "You've saved me a lot of hard digging."

"Hurray," shouted the bunnies. "We've got some treasure after all."

**D**anny was a deep sea diver. He had a wet suit, a face mask, and flippers. On his back were two air bottles so he could breathe under water.

Desmond was exploring the sea bed. He was hunting for pearls. Schools of fish swam by. They were all the colors of the rainbow.

But Danny couldn't find any pearls. "Never mind," he said. "I'll take back some coral."

Danny swam toward a pink rock. Suddenly a huge octopus appeared. He grabbed Danny with all his eight arms and squeezed him tighter and tighter.

"Let go," cried Danny. "Help! Help!"

"Wake up," said the octopus.

But it wasn't the octopus at all. It was Danny's mother. She was pulling him out of bed.

"There's no time for dreaming," said his mother firmly. "You'll be late for school. And don't forget your swim suit. You've got a swimming lesson today."

# THE SECRET TUNNEL

Ollie and Biff were building a secret tunnel in the garden. They borrowed the kitchen chairs and some old sheets, and their father gave them some big cardboard boxes.

They turned the chairs upside down, put them in a long line, and hung the sheets over them. Then Biff tore the bottoms out of the boxes, and they lined them up to make a long tunnel. When the tunnel was finished, their father gave them some donuts. "You'll need these if it's a very long tunnel," he said. "You might get hungry."

Biff went first, and Ollie followed. It took a long time to travel through the tunnel. Ollie kept getting his head stuck in the bars of the chairs and had to be rescued, and Biff couldn't see where he was going, because it was too dark.

"Where did your tunnel lead to?" said their father, when they had reached the end.

"We can't tell you that!" said the little bunnies. "It's a secret tunnel!"

**R**ussell loved his roller skates. He never took them off. He wore them to play. He wore them at mealtimes. He even wore them to bed!

One day, Russell went to the park. First he skated over to the seesaw. Up and down he went — wearing his skates.

Next, he skated up to the merry-go-round. Round and round he went — skates and all.

Then, he made for the slide. He clattered up the steps with his skates. Then he whizzed down.

But at the bottom, Russell didn't stop. He went on . . . and on . . . and on.

At the far edge of the park was a duck pond. "Oh, no," said Russell as he zoomed closer and closer.

Russell landed right in the middle of the pond. The ducks were very angry with him.

When Russell got home, he asked his mother to dry his wet clothes.

"Of, course, dear," replied his mother. "We'll start with your roller skates!"

T

oday," said Mother Rabbit, "we're going to make bunny cookies."

She put Baby Rabbit in his high chair and gave him a bowl and a small wooden spoon. She gave Max a larger bowl and a large wooden spoon.

She weighed out the flour, butter, and sugar. "You mix it all up like this," she said, and they tried to copy her.

Max and Baby Rabbit mixed and mixed. Baby Rabbit got his nose and ears covered in the mixture, and when he sneezed the mixture flew all over the kitchen.

"Oh dear," said Mother Rabbit.

Mother Rabbit showed Max how to roll his mixture out flat, and to cut out bunny shapes with the cutter. She rolled Baby's mixture out flat, but he dropped it on the floor.

"Oh dear," said Mother Rabbit.

Suddenly, Max began to cry. "My bunny's got no eyes!" he wailed.

"Oh dear," said Mother Rabbit.

Mother Rabbit gave Max some raisins for the eyes, and some orange peel for the whiskers.

At last, the cookies were ready. In fact, they looked so perfect, neither Mother Rabbit, nor Baby Rabbit, nor Max had the heart to eat them!

There was always trouble when it was peas for supper. Ted hated them. Once, he hid some under his plate; once, he even put his peas on his mother's plate when she wasn't looking; once, he dropped them on the floor and the cat stepped on them; once, he flicked them at his sister. And once, he made such a fuss that his mother took his plate away altogether.

"I hate peas," Ted would say. "They're like caterpillars' eggs."

One day, when they were out shopping, Ted pointed out some long green pods. "What are those?" he asked.

"Those are peas," said his mother.

"No, they're not. Peas are round and look like caterpillars' eggs."

Ted's mother bought some pods. She showed Ted how to open them. Inside the pods were rows of shiny green peas.

"These aren't caterpillars' eggs," said Ted. "They're precious green pearls." And he ate a whole plateful for his supper.

**I** don't want to move house," sobbed Rosemary.

Her parents tried to comfort her. "The bedrooms in the new house are bigger than the ones here," said her mother.

"We'll have our own cabbage patch," said her father.

"I don't want a bigger bedroom. And I don't like cabbage," cried Rosemary.

Eventually, it was moving day. When Rosemary arrived at the new house, she trailed through the little gate. Next to the cabbage patch was a swing. "That's nice," said Rosemary, "but I won't like my room."

At bedtime, Rosemary found a door with her name on it. She peeked inside. Everything had been carefully arranged. It looked just like her room at the old house. There were some extra things too — a little wash basin, a new cushion, and a fluffy mouse.

Rosemary's face lit up. "I like it after all," she said. She turned to her parents shyly. "I might even try some cabbage tomorrow."

**L**ongears wanted to be the best at everything.

"When I grow up, I'll be the biggest, bravest, smartest, strongest, fastest bunny in the world," he said.

Longears ran out to play with the other bunnies. He won all the races and he could jump and hop farther than anyone. When the others stopped to rest or nibble the grass, Longears kept on running.

One small bunny hopped over to him. "I don't know how you'll ever be the biggest bunny in the world, when you never stop to eat anything," she said.

So Longears began to nibble the grass. When the other bunnies played again, he kept on eating. He ate and ate. He ate all morning and all afternoon. "I *will* be the biggest bunny in the world," he said.

Much later, the small bunny caught sight of him. "Hello, biggest, bravest, smartest, strongest, fastest bunny in the whole world," she said. "Let's have a race."

Poor Longears was so full, he could hardly hop at all. The small bunny won easily.

Longears crawled home, exhausted. "Well," he said, "nobody can be the best at *everything*."

I t was Alan's birthday. He wanted a party. His mother was dreading it because all Alan's friends were so lively and noisy. "How will I amuse them?" she wondered.

"Don't worry," said Alan's father. "You buy the food; I'll arrange the games."

Alan's mother went into town. She tried to keep her mind on the shopping, but she kept thinking about all those rabbits and what she was going to do with them. She lost all track of time, and when she got home, the party had already started.

No one had missed Alan's mother. Alan was bouncing and shrieking. So were all his friends. But they weren't bouncing on the furniture. Alan's Dad had rented a bouncy castle. The castle was taking all the knocks. All Alan's mother had to do was to put out the food.

"What an invention!" cried Alan's mother. "It must have been made by someone very smart — with children just like Alan!"

**M**o was fed up. He didn't know what to do. He tried to play with his garage, but his favorite car was broken. He tried to color in a picture, but all his coloring pens had dried up. He went into the yard to play football, but his ball had a puncture. Mo sat on the ground and began to cry.

Then he noticed a long line of ants marching along the ground. The ants looked very busy. They were carrying small leaves and seeds. Mo sat and watched the ants for a long time.

"What are the ants doing?" asked Mo, when his father came to get him.

"They're busy collecting food. They're working," Mo's father replied.

"I wish I had some work to do," sighed the little bunny.

"You can come and help me," said his father.

Mo's father showed him how to sweep up, and how to dry all the spoons and plates and put them away.

"I like working," said Mo.

"Good," said Mo's father. "But now that we've finished, I'd like to play!"

**D**onald was depressed. He had a cold. He was going to miss the air show. "I want to see dose planes," said Donald, wiping his nose.

"You must stay indoors until you are better," said his mother.

Donald sulked. "Don't want dany doast," he said, when his mother brought breakfast.

All morning Donald's father was busy. Then he left for the air show. "You can watch from your window," he said.

"Won't be dable to dee danything," said Donald.

Donald's mother persuaded him to sit by the window. They could see the planes in the distance. What smart pilots they were! They flew high and low, upside down and right side up. Donald soon forgot his cold.

Suddenly, one of the planes flew toward them. It was trailing a large banner. Donald could read the words clearly. They said, "GET WELL SOON, DONALD."

"Good dold Dad," cried Donald happily. "So dats what he was doing dall dorning!"

Father Rabbit was taking Josh and Laurie shopping. Instead of walking properly, the two little bunnies kept taking huge steps, and jumping about all over the place.

"What are you two doing?" asked their father.

"We're trying not to step on the lines on the sidewalk," said Josh.

"If we do, a great big bear will gobble us up," added Laurie.

"Well," said Father Rabbit, "I know what'll happen if you don't walk properly. A terrible Muzzlewop will grab you instead!"

"What's a Muzzlewop?" asked Laurie.

"It's huge and hairy, and has long ears and a very big growl, like this," said Father Rabbit, growling and chasing the two little rabbits along the road.

"What else does a Muzzlewop do?" asked Josh.

"Oh," said Father Rabbit, "lots of things. It takes you shopping, it buys you toys if you are good, and it tucks you up in bed at night."

"That sounds just like . . . our daddy!" laughed Josh and Laurie, giving Father Rabbit a big hug.

**I**ke Rabbit loved food. He ate at least six meals a day. No wonder he was getting tubby!

One day Ike was playing hide-and-seek with his friends. He knew the ideal hiding place — a hollow oak. But to get to it he had to squeeze under a gate. He squeezed and he squeezed, but his tummy was too round. He was stuck!

In the distance Ike heard his friends shouting, "We're coming to get you, Fatty" — but they never did "get" him, because who would think of a *gate* as a hiding place?

Poor Ike. The next two days were the loneliest, hungriest days of his life. But by the third day, he had gotten thin enough to work himself free!

"I *much* prefer being slim," Ike thought, admiring his reflection in a puddle. "From now on I'm going to eat sensibly."

Even though Ike had promised not to eat so much in future, he did treat himself to a giant-sized peanut butter sandwich when he got home. Well, I think he deserved it, don't you?

# THE MAGIC RUG

It was a cold winter's afternoon. It was too cold to play outside, and Jody and Tom were sitting in front of the fire with Grandma Rabbit.

"I wish we could go somewhere," said Tom.

"We could go somewhere on this magic rug," said Grandma. "Close your eyes tight. Where should we go?"

"To the park," said Tom.

"To the North Pole," shouted Jody.

"We'll go to the park first," said Grandma. "Close your eyes. Off we go. There's the pond, down there. It's frozen over. The ducks look cold and wet. Hold on tight. We'll go to the North Pole now. Nearly there. What can you see?"

"Snow," said Jody. "Lots and lots of snow."

"And lots of polar bears," said Tom, "and icebergs."

"It's freezing," said Jody. "Let's go home."

"Hold on tight, then," said their grandmother. "Here we are. Home again. Where should we go now?"

"Let's just stay at home for a while," said Tom. "It's warmer here!"

**H**opalong Rabbit was the fastest draw in the woods. He lived in a pretend world of cowboys and Indians. He hid behind trees and shot at his friends.

His gun was loaded with rubber pellets, not bullets. But they still hurt. Hopalong was a menace.

One day he was hiding in the woods when along came his friend Speedy the tortoise.

Hopalong rubbed his hands with glee. He reached for his holster. He flicked his wrist and twirled his gun. "Ping!" The pellet hit Speedy fair and square.

"Bull's-eye!" cried Hopalong cheerfully.

But he spoke too soon. The pellet bounced right off Speedy's shell and back on to Hopalong's nose. "Ow, ow, ouch," he cried.

"Serves you right," said Speedy. "Now you know what it feels like when people shoot things at you."

Hopalong's nose was swollen for days. He decided to hang up his gun. Or maybe . . . he could swop it for a water pistol?

**L**izzie and Ellie were helping their father tidy the garden shed. Everything was in a terrible mess. There were empty paint pots, old toys, broken flowerpots, rusty tools, and lots of bits of wood.

Lizzie and Ellie sorted out all the rusty nails, hooks, screws, and nuts and bolts into separate cans, while their father hung up the tools and threw out the things he didn't need any more.

Father Rabbit was just about to throw away some old wood when Lizzie stopped him. "Don't throw that out, Daddy," she said. "We can make something with it."

Father Rabbit gave Lizzie and Ellie the wood, and some nails and hammers too. While he finished sweeping and cleaning the shed, Lizzie and Ellie began hammering and banging and sawing. They made a great, huge Thing.

"That's very nice," said their father, when they had finished. "But it's too big to go in your bedroom."

"We know!" said Ellie. "There's so much room in your shed now, we can keep it in there!"

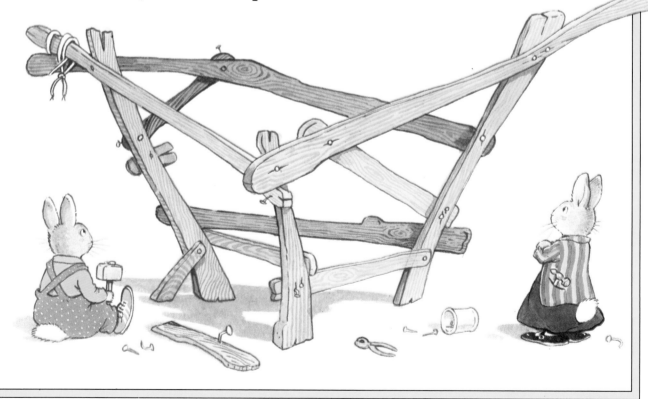

**R**on and Ruby liked to play jokes on each other.

One day Ron put a mouse in Ruby's bed. The next, Ruby laced Ron's drink with mustard.

"Ugh! I'll get my own back," spluttered Ron.

Ron waited till midnight. Then he climbed quietly out of bed. He took off the sheet and wrapped it around him. He was going to pretend he was a ghost.

"Whooh, whooh," he howled, as he felt his way across the landing.

"Whooh, whooh," came the reply.

Ron stopped in his tracks. He peeked round the edge of his sheet. He could see a white shape. It was still making whooh whooh noises.

Ron didn't believe in ghosts. Or did he? He began to feel frightened. Then he looked closer. There was something odd about the shape. And that voice.

Oh, no! It was Ruby. She had thought up exactly the same idea as Ron!

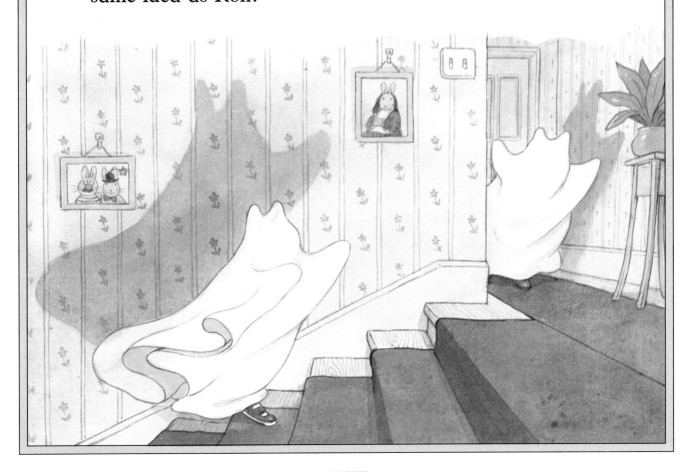

**L**udwig van Rabbit was a famous pianist. All day long he played the piano. The trouble was, he *never* stopped playing . . .

"Can you fix my train, Daddy?" said Hans. But there was no reply from Ludwig.

"Look at my picture, Daddy," said Heidi. But Ludwig didn't look.

"Ludwig, please help me wash the dishes," said his wife. But Ludwig didn't hear.

Then Ludwig's family hit on a plan. Every time they spoke to him, they would sing.

"Doh, ray, me, fah, soh, it's nearly time to go," sang Hans, when he needed Ludwig to take him to school.

"La, la, la, la, please fix my guitar," sang Heidi, when she broke her guitar string.

"Pom pom, pom pom, the mailman's come," sang his wife, when she brought in the mail.

The plan worked. Ludwig loved the musical messages. And, at last, he began to take notice of his family.

One suppertime Chris wouldn't eat his vegetables, so his mother sent him to bed early. "Small rabbits should eat what's put in front of them," she said.

That night, Chris decided to run away. He made a little bag and tied it to a stick. He tucked his teddy bear into the bag and set off. The bright moon lit the way.

"This is fun," said Chris. He strode farther and farther from home.

Suddenly, the moon went behind a cloud. Then, it began to rain. Eventually, Chris found a barn to sleep in.

"I feel so lonely," he sobbed, "even with my teddy bear."

The next morning, Chris set off for home. It took such a long time to get there. He was very tired, and he kept getting lost.

Chris's mother was very worried. Where could Chris have gone?

At last Chris reached home. His mother was very relieved. She made lunch right away. And Chris was so hungry — he ate up *all* his greens!

**S**omething was wrong in Bluebell Wood. Every night there was a dreadful noise. The rabbits couldn't get to sleep.

Night after night the noise would start. Could it be a monster? Everyone knew that monsters came out at night.

Little bunnies stayed indoors after dark, while their parents tried to soothe them to sleep. But still the noise went on.

The adult rabbits had a meeting, and decided to investigate the noise. They set off bravely.

The noise grew louder and nearer. What a din! And what a surprise for the rabbits!

The noise wasn't being made by a monster at all. It was Hamish McFox. He was playing the bagpipes!

Hamish looked sheepish. "I get homesick for Scotland," he said. "I didn't think you would hear me in your sleep."

"That's all right, Hamish," said the rabbits. "We'll all sleep soundly, now we know what the noise is!"

**W**hy are we bothering to go fishing?" John asked his friend Sam. "We'll never catch anything with these home-made rods and no bait."

"We might be lucky," said Sam. "Come on."

So they went to the river, cast off and waited . . . and waited . . . and waited.

"This is boring," said John. "I wish we were playing football."

Suddenly, Sam felt a tug on his rod. "I think I've caught a fish!" he cried, yanking up his rod. Hanging from the hook was a wet, torn, purple box.

"That's the funniest fish I've ever seen," said John sulkily.

Sam tore open the box. "It's Mrs. Brown's diamond necklace!" he said. "Do you remember, she was burgled and offered a reward for its safe return?"

They hurried round to Mrs. Brown's house. She was so delighted to have the necklace back she divided the reward between them.

John spent his money on a new football. But Sam spent his on a gleaming new fishing rod and some bait!

et's play monsters," said Joe.

"Great," said Charlie. "Let's get dressed up."

They went to the old dressing up box. There were old hats, old scarves, bits of material, dresses, aprons, and a black velvet jacket, which was Joe's favorite.

Joe grabbed the velvet jacket. "I'm using this," he said.

"I wanted that," said Charlie, pouting. "Black is the scariest color, and it's the only black thing here."

"But it's mine," said Joe. "I always wear it." He held out a long red scarf for Charlie. "You can wear this. Red's scary too."

Charlie sulked. Then, he noticed a green silk scarf. It looked just like a snake. And then he had an idea.

When Joe wasn't looking, Charlie crept quietly to a corner of the room. He held the scarf at one end and slowly wriggled it as he went. When Joe looked round, all he saw was a green snake slithering across the room.

"Help! Help!" called Joe. "There's a snake in my room."

"See," laughed Charlie. "Black and red aren't the scariest colors after all. The scariest color of all is green!"

It was a hot summer's night. Willie and Jess were lying in bed, tossing and turning.

"Keep still, Willie," said Jess.

"I can't," said Willie. "I'm too hot. Mom," he called, "Mom, I can't get to sleep."

Willie and Jess's mother came upstairs. "Okay," she said. "I'll tell you a story. Then you have to go to sleep.

"Once upon a time, in a hot, hot country, there was a hot, hot desert. The hot, hot sun shone down on the hot, hot sand. It was so hot, you could fry an egg on the ground."

"Phew," said Willie. "I'm glad it's not that hot here."

"Shh," their mother went on. "The hot, hot sun shone down. It shone and shone all day. Everything sizzled and baked and frizzled and fried on the hot, hot sand in that hot, hot desert, in that hot, hot . . ."

She looked down. Both little bunnies were fast asleep.

**L**ong ago, there lived an enormous rabbit called Giant Long Ears. Giant Long Ears loved playing hide-and-seek. One day he asked five baby rabbits to play with him. He promised to give a basket of carrots to the rabbit who stayed hidden the longest.

Giant Long Ears closed his eyes and began to count. The baby rabbits ran off in all directions. One hid in a barn, another in a field of cabbages, another hid in the farmhouse, another in the hen-house. But one baby rabbit could not find anywhere to hide.

"Ninety-seven, ninety-eight..." roared Giant Long Ears. Time was nearly up.

Suddenly, the baby rabbit had an idea. With a quick hop, he jumped right inside Giant Long Ears' coat pocket.

"One hundred! I'm coming," bellowed Giant Long Ears.

One by one, he found four baby rabbits. But he could not find the fifth rabbit anywhere. He searched and searched over fields and mountains. Finally he sat down, exhausted.

"I give up," he roared. And out of his pockets crept the little baby rabbit, to claim her prize.

**N**orman had been invited to a costume party, but he had nothing to wear.

Mary was going as Cinderella. Her mother had made her a lovely ballgown.

Eddie was going as a clown. He had a bright silk shirt and a floppy hat.

Carmen was going as a fairy. Her mother had made her a wispy skirt with little net wings to match.

But Norman's mother couldn't sew.

Then she had a great idea. She got an old tablecloth and some Christmas streamers. The tablecloth was orange, and the streamers were green.

She wrapped the tablecloth around Norman and tied it in a knot on top of his head. Then she cut two slits in the cloth for his eyes.

Next, she started to work with the streamers.

When she was finished, Norman wriggled over to the mirror. He peered through the slits in the tablecloth.

And what a surprise he got. He looked just like a giant carrot!

ax and Sadie loved collecting horse chestnuts. Max liked polishing their hard shells and sorting them into piles. Sadie liked taking hers to school for horse chestnut fights.

One morning, Max and Sadie went to the park to find horse chestnuts. They found lots and lots, but they soon began to quarrel.

"That's mine," said Sadie.

"I saw it first," said Max.

Then Mother Rabbit said, "We'll put them all into one bag, and then I'll give you equal amounts."

When the little bunnies had collected all the horse chestnuts they could find, Mother Rabbit tipped out the bag and began to make two piles.

"One for you, Sadie, and one for you, Max..." she said, as she counted them out.

Soon both rabbits had exactly the same amount of horse chestnuts — but there was one left over.

"What should we do with that one?" asked Max.

"I know," said Sadie. "We'll plant it. Then, one day there'll be a brand new horse chestnut tree — and lots and lots more horse chestnuts!"

**M**ichael was a clever magician. He could do all kinds of tricks. If you took a card from his pack, he could guess what it was. If you gave him your handkerchief, he could tie it in knots — without touching. He could even make things disappear.

But there was one trick Michael could not get right. Michael had a mouse called Miles. Miles was meant to appear out of his hat. But he always turned up late.

Michael had a talk with Miles. It was time to sort things out. Miles explained the problem.

"I see," said Michael. "I'll try to remember."

That night, Michael took off his hat. "I will now say the magic word," he said. And he said it.

Miles appeared out of the hat right on cue. He looked at Michael and winked.

The trick was easy. Instead of "Abracadabra," the magic word Malcolm used was "Please!"

**I**t was a hot night. Robert and Joanie couldn't sleep. "Let's go exploring," whispered Robert. "If we creep out very quietly, Mom and Dad won't hear us."

So they did. It was the first time they had been outside at night. How different everything looked. All those shadows... and the strange rustling noises that during the day wouldn't bother you at all. They crept along the hedge. In the distance they heard a bark — could it be a fox?

"Let's go home," said Joanie. "I'm frightened."

Suddenly, a dark shadow fell over them. They looked up. It was an owl! The bunnies froze. Their parents had told them all about owls — about their fantastic eyesight and sharp claws and beaks, and how they liked nothing better than baby rabbit for dinner.

Had the owl seen them? Surely it could hear the thump of their hearts! For what seemed like hours, it hovered above them. Then it flew silently away.

For the rest of the night, Robert and Joanie hid under the hedge. It wasn't until daybreak that they dared go home.

"Breakfast's ready, children," called their father as they crept back into bed. So they hadn't been missed! But they vowed never again to go out at night — well, not until they were much older.

**S**andra crept into her parents' bed to open her Christmas stocking.

She rummaged about in the foot, and pulled out a sugar carrot. She would eat it after lunch.

Then she felt inside the toe, and pulled out a pack of cards.

"Oooh, can we play cards now?" asked Sandra.

"When we're awake," said her parents, sleepily.

In the leg of the stocking were two large parcels. Sandra shivered with excitement as she unwrapped them. The first was a box of paints.

"Can I paint now?" asked Sandra.

"After breakfast," said her parents, sleepily.

In the last parcel was a lovely rag bunny. "It's what I've always wanted," said Sandra.

"And now for one last present," said her parents.

They sat up in bed and gave her a great... big... HUG.

"Mmmm, thank you,' said Sandra. "That was the best present of all!"

# THE SCHOOL TRIP

The bunnies at Burrow High were excited. It was the day of the school trip.

Miss Hopmore had chartered a bus. They were all going to visit an old castle. The bunnies had learnt all about castles in their history lessons.

"No standing on the seats!" said Miss Hopmore. "And save your sandwiches for later."

At the castle Miss Hopmore had her hands full. Melvyn fell in the moat, George lowered the drawbridge, and Larry hid inside a suit of armor.

Then Linda tore her dress, and clumsy Dolores sat in a cow pat.

At the end of the day, Miss Hopmore counted the bunnies as they climbed back onto the bus.

"Thank goodness!" she said, wiping her brow. "All present and correct."

The pupils of Burrow High sang all the way home. Miss Hopmore put cotton balls in her ears.

Finally, they were back at the school gates and all the parents were waiting to meet them.

"We've had a wonderful day," said Miss Hopmore. "Tomorrow the children can write all about it in school. And I can have a rest!"

**R**odney was a television fan. Whatever program was on, Rodney wanted to see it.

Rodney's friends called by to play. "I'll come out when the TV has finished," said Rodney. But he never went.

"Supper's ready," called his mother. Rodney stole back to the television with his supper on a tray.

"That boy will get square eyes," said his father.

Then one day, a wonderful thing happened. The television set broke down.

Rodney's mother seized her chance. She took Rodney to the library and, together, they chose some books. Then she took him ice skating. And after, they went and bought some carrot burgers — and ate them all.

Last of all, Rodney's mother took him to the pet store, and bought him a parrot called Percy.

"I'll teach Percy to talk," said Rodney.

The next day the television repair man came. "Take your time," Rodney told him politely. "I'm far too busy to watch TV now."

**H**ector Hare sold delicious ice-cream. He made it himself with butter, cream, and sugar. Then he added *Hare's Secret Ingredient*.

"Hector's ice-cream, Hector's ice-cream," he would shout, and the customers would come running.

It was a long, hot summer, and Hector's business was flourishing.

Then, one day, Hector's mixer broke down. Hector was in a panic. How could he make enough ice-cream?

The woodland bunnies came to the rescue. They offered to mix the ice-cream by hand. "Many hands make light work," they said.

"Thanks a lot," said Hector. But he made them close their eyes whenever he added his secret ingredient.

What a success! Hector was able to keep his customers happy. The bunnies kept out of mischief, and they were allowed to lick their paws whenever they wanted.

As soon as he had time, Hector put up a new sign:
HECTOR'S SPECIALTY ICE-CREAM —
NOW MIXED ONLY BY HAND!

## RANDY ROBOT

**R**andy was a robot. He belonged to the Rabbit-Smiths. He washed their dishes, he made their beds, he chopped their logs.

One day, things began to go wrong. Randy dropped some plates. Then he tore the sheets. And then he cut his tin finger on the chopper.

"What's wrong, Randy?" said Mrs. Rabbit-Smith.

"It's no good having a robot who makes a mess of things," said Mr. Rabbit-Smith.

They looked in the instruction booklet. "Maybe Randy's joints need oiling?" said Mrs. Rabbit-Smith.

"Maybe we should get him serviced?" said her husband.

At supper time, Randy was missing. The Rabbit-Smiths found him lying on his bed. He was reading a holiday brochure.

"Now I know what's wrong," smiled Mrs. Rabbit-Smith. "Randy needs a break. We should send him on a holiday. And then *you* can help me with the chores," she told her husband!

**L**ong Ears was out hunting in the forest because his food supply was running low. In the distance was a woolly mammoth.

"Mmm, mammoth steak," thought Long Ears, and his mouth began to water.

He set off in pursuit. But when he got closer, he didn't feel so hungry. This was a *very large* mammoth. And Long Ears had only a *very small* club.

Long Ears decided to go fishing instead. He waited by the stream. Every so often a fish flew up out of the water. But Long Ears just couldn't catch one.

"What a day!" he thought. He walked sadly home, dragging his club behind him.

"Have you had any luck?" asked Myrtle, his wife.

"None at all," said Long Ears. "But what's that delicious smell?"

"That's stew," said Myrtle. "I made it from some funny orange things that the children found outside."

And that was the first time ever that rabbits had carrot stew for supper!

**R**obert had invited his sister over to supper, so he decided to bake a loaf of bread. "I haven't got a recipe, but never mind," he said to himself. "I'm sure all you do is mix together flour, salt, yeast and water, shove it in the oven — and there you are!"

Which was exactly what he did. Then he went off to buy some cakes.

What Robert didn't realize was that you only need a very small amount of yeast to make bread. He had put in handfuls! So, like Jack's beanstalk, the bread began to grow and grow. It grew around the sides of the oven door, across the kitchen, and through the window!

When Robert returned, he couldn't believe his eyes. There was bread growing all over his yard.

"Oh well. I'd better buy some more cakes and invite the whole village to supper, instead of just my sister," he said.

And he did. What a good time was had by all. And there was certainly no shortage of bread!

**B**enjamin, Brian, and Bruce went out in a boat, fishing.

Benjamin was the first to feel a tug on his line. "This is it," he said.

But it wasn't a fish. It was an old umbrella. "Never mind," said Benjamin. "I've always wanted an umbrella. I'll dry it out and save it for a rainy day."

Very soon Brian felt a tug on *his* line. "Here we go," he said.

But it wasn't a fish. It was an old trumpet. "Never mind," said Brian. "I'll become a musician. I can dry out this trumpet and take lessons."

Not long after, Bruce felt a tug on *his* line. "Look out!" said Bruce.

But it wasn't a fish. It was an old saucepan.

"Never mind," said Bruce. "Let's brew carrot wine in my saucepan. We can invite our friends to try it — and tell them all about our fishing adventures!"

**I**t had been snowing all night long. The girls wanted to play. But Mrs. Rabbit was a worrier.

"*Please* can we go out to play?" cried Dinah and Donna.

"No!" said Mrs. Rabbit, firmly. "The snow's too deep."

"I want to make a snow bunny," said Dinah.

"I want to throw snowballs," said Donna.

It was not long before the other animals went out to play in the snow.

"Look," pointed Dinah, "there's Fergus Frog."

"And Sydney Squirrel," shouted Donna.

Dinah sobbed. Donna pleaded. They wanted so badly to go out and play.

All of a sudden Mrs. Rabbit knew what to do. She looked in her knitting bag and brought out some bright red pom-poms. She tied them to her daughters' ears and sent them out to play.

That way, everyone was happy. The girls were delighted to be in the snow at last. And Mrs. Rabbit knew they were safe, because she could see the pom-poms dancing from her window.

**P**rudence was Polly's china piggy bank. She was decorated with pink flowers. She had a large slit in the middle of her back to take the coins. And she had a rubber stopper in her tummy. That's where the coins came out.

Polly shook Prudence gently. She wanted to get out some money.

"You should save your money for something special," said Polly's mother. But Polly needed money *now*.

She waited until her parents were asleep. Then she opened the stopper in Prudence's tummy and took out several coins. Then she fell asleep, with a smile on her face.

The next day was her mother's birthday. Polly came running into the house. She held out a big potted plant.

"Oh, Polly," said her mother, "you shouldn't have spent all your money on me!"

"Oh yes I should," said Polly. "You told me to save it for something *special*!"

**D**ennis wanted to be a detective. He was always looking for clues. He spent his time tailing people and searching for paw prints. He couldn't wait for a crime to take place.

One day, there was a real mystery in the woods. A sack of carrots had been stolen from Spring Cottage.

"A rabbit riddle at last!" said Dennis, and rushed to the scene of the crime.

Dennis took out his magnifying glass. He peered at the ground outside Spring Cottage. "Aha, what's this?" cried Dennis, as he picked up a shiny button.

Then he saw some paw prints. They led to Gobble Cottage, the home of Tubby Feedmore.

Dennis found Tubby tucking into a huge pile of carrots. And his top vest button was missing. Dennis had caught Tubby red-handed!

The rabbits at Spring Cottage were so delighted, they invited Dennis to supper.

"Yes, please!" said Dennis. "This detective work can make you very hungry."

Once there was a young rabbit who was learning to be a wizard. He loved trying out his magic, but his father warned him, "You must use your magic carefully. Don't waste it, or you may use it all up."

But the little rabbit loved showing off his new tricks. He could make a marble roll uphill; he could empty a glass of water without touching it; he could even make himself disappear into thin air.

One day, the little rabbit had been showing off his magic more than ever when he waved his wand for just one more trick . . .

Nothing happened!

The little rabbit's friends began to laugh, and he ran home.

"I'm afraid you've used up all your magic," said his father.

"Will it ever come back?" sobbed the little rabbit.

"It will, in time," said his father, "when you are older and wiser, and have learned to say 'no more!'"

**L**eroy was a lion tamer. The lions loved him. Each year he thought up a new act for them. One year they leapt through a hoop. The next, they dribbled a basketball.

"What act are you going to perform this year?" asked the circus boss.

Leroy didn't know. He was running short of ideas. He climbed up on the high trapeze to have a think.

High in the big top, Leroy had a brainwave...

That year, Leroy trained the lions harder than ever. At last the new act was ready. The band played a lively tune, and the lions romped into the ring.

The audience looked puzzled. What were the lions wearing? They looked ready for bed.

Suddenly, the lions sprang into action. The audience couldn't believe their eyes. The lions were doing *judo*.

When the circus boss heard the cheers, he made up his mind at once. "Leroy, this act is the tops," he said. "You mustn't change it for years."

**I**t was time to wash the dishes, and Freddy and Freda were fighting. "It's your turn to dry," each one was shouting at the other.

The same thing happened every day. It made their mother angry.

"That's enough," she said one day. "I've decided what to do."

Freddy and Freda's mother put a chart on the wall. She gave Freddy a blue crayon and Freda a red one.

"Listen carefully," she said. "This chart shows the days of the week. It has a space for all our meals. Whoever dries the dishes can crayon in the space. Don't forget, blue for Freddy, red for Freda. Then we'll know where we are."

"What a terrific idea!" said Freddy and Freda together. They couldn't wait to start.

They still thought it was boring to dry the dishes. But it was such fun filling in the chart.

Their mother was pleased too. "Thank goodness," she said. "At last we'll have *no more arguments*!"

Superbunny looked down from the rooftop. Those wicked rabbits were at it again. Last week they had robbed a bank. The week before that they had kidnapped a film star. Now it looked as if they were after the toy store. "They'll never learn," sighed Superbunny to himself.

He decided to wait until the rabbit robbers were inside the store. Then he would fly down and catch them red-handed.

"Now!" said Superbunny to himself. He spread out his cloak and leapt from the roof of the skyscraper.

Down and down he went. He would catch those robbers in no time at all.

"THUD!" Superbunny had made a crash landing . . .

"Ernie," cried a voice from the kitchen. "How many times have I told you? No jumping down all those stairs at once!"

"Sorry Mom,' said Ernie. "But what else can a rabbit do when it's raining? And it's such fun being brave, fearless Superbunny!"

123

Ethel had toothache. Her mother looked inside her mouth and prodded gently. "Ouch, that hurts," said Ethel.

Ethel's father came home from work. He looked inside Ethel's mouth as she opened wide. "Ouch, that hurts," said Ethel.

Ethel's parents couldn't see anything wrong. So they took her to the dentist.

"Sit down, Ethel," said the dentist, kindly. He looked carefully right inside Ethel's mouth, while Ethel tried to tell him where it hurt. He touched the gum at the back. "Ouch, that hurts," said Ethel.

The dentist smiled at Ethel. "Your teeth are fine," he said. "I can see you brush them well."

Ethel's parents glowed with pride.

"But you're growing an extra tooth at the back," he added. "Some rabbits do. It's called a wisdom tooth. It will soon be through. Then it won't hurt any more."

Ethel felt important, now she had a wisdom tooth. "Will I come top of the class?" she asked. "Now that I have a *wisdom* tooth!"

**L**ofty and Shorty were best friends. No one could understand why.

Lofty was the tallest boy in the whole school. Shorty was the smallest.

When they went to the movies Shortie would tip up his seat, to make him as tall as Lofty.

When they played football, Lofty would pass the ball to Shorty. Shorty would lob it up in the air, and Lofty would run in a touchdown. They made a winning team.

When they played the piano, Lofty would take the high notes, and Shorty the low notes. They made sweet music together.

When Lofty felt lazy Shorty would tie his shoelaces, because he was so much nearer to Lofty's feet. If Shorty wanted a rest, Lofty would get down his coat. It was no reach at all.

Lofty and Shorty knew what people said. "There goes the long and the short of it."

But they didn't mind at all. Because, inside, they knew they were a perfect match.

The English Country Bunkins were going to London. They had never been to a town before.

The bus dropped them at Buckingham Palace. The noise of the traffic was deafening. The Country Bunkins stuffed cotton balls in their ears as they watched the changing of the guard.

They took a taxi to the Tower of London and climbed right to the top. It made them feel dizzy to look down.

They caught the subway to Trafalgar Square. The subway train was fun, but very dirty. The Country Bunkins rushed out into the fresh air and fed the pigeons carrot sandwiches.

The Country Bunkins looked at their watches. They would have to hurry to catch their bus.

"Tell me what you've done," said the bus driver.

"We got *deafened*, *dizzy*, and *dirty*," said the Country Bunkins. "We saw lots of new things — but we can't wait to get back to the country!"

# PLAY IT AGAIN, LUKE

Luke wanted to be a pop star. He wore tight pants and dark glasses. He bought an old guitar and strummed it night and day.

Luke's parents didn't like the noise, and they didn't like the way he dressed.

"I wish you'd have a talk with Luke," said his mother.

"Boys will be boys," sighed his father.

One night, a burglar broke into Luke's house. His parents were asleep, but Luke heard the noise. He'd stayed awake, composing a tune.

Luke crept downstairs. He took his guitar with him.

"CRASH!" Luke banged his guitar over the burglar's head.

Luke's guitar had broken into pieces, but the burglar was out cold. Luke called the police.

"We've been after this burglar for months," said the Chief of Police. "There will be quite a reward."

"Hurray!" said Luke. "I'll buy a new guitar — and play it right away!"

**L**ittle Rabbit was sitting among the clover, gazing up at the big hill. Some bunnies said that a million foxes lived there; others said there was a pack of terrible wolves. "I wish I knew what happened on the other side of the hill," sighed Little Rabbit.

Old Wise Bunny was strolling nearby. He saw Little Rabbit looking glumly at the hill. "What's the matter with you?" he said.

"I want to know what happens on the other side of the hill," replied Little Rabbit.

"That's easy," said Old Wise Bunny. "Over the hill is where the sun goes to bed."

Little Rabbit sat and waited. He watched the sun slowly sinking in the sky until, at last, it disappeared behind the big hill.

"It *is* where the sun goes to bed!" cried Little Rabbit. "Now I know what happens on the other side of the hill."

And Little Rabbit ran happily all the way home to get ready for *his* bed.